Secret Star

Secret Star

NANCY SPRINGER

PHILOMEL BOOKS ♦ NEW YORK

Library of Congress Cataloging-in-Publication Data
Springer, Nancy. Secret Star / by Nancy Springer.   p.   cm.
Summary: Fourteen years old, dirt-poor, and unable to remember
anything that happened to her before she was ten, Tess is happy
living with her wheelchair-bound stepfather, until a scarred young
man finds her and starts asking questions about her "real" father.
[1. Stepfathers—Fiction. 2. Amnesia—Fiction. 3. Poverty—Fiction.
4. Physically handicapped—Fiction.] I. Title.   PZ7.S76846Se   1997
[Fic]—dc20   96-12091   CIP   AC   ISBN 0-399-23028-9 (hardcover)
10   9   8   7   6   5   4   3   2   1   First Impression

To Jim

Nobody tells you when you're going to meet the cross-roads person. Nobody tells you when life is going to pick you up by the ankles. As far as Tess knew, it was just another April weekday and she was just weird Tess Mathis.

She was hiking home across country the way she usually did, because she didn't enjoy sitting alone on the school bus and she loved the creek country in the springtime. The brown butterflies with blue fringes were out, violets were pushing up, and Tess was playing music inside her head. So what if Daddy hadn't been able to pay the bill, and a man in gray coveralls had come and shut off the electricity, and Tess missed radio more than she missed having lights at night. Fourteen years old and she didn't have diddley—no money, no boobs, no boyfriend, no smiley faces on her report cards, no Walkman no stereo no MTV—but yes she still had music inside her, riffs and rhythms that belonged to no one else. Nothing and nobody could take that away.

So Tess stomped along in her old Red Wing work boots, humming, slapping and tapping out time with her chunky fingers on her thighs, not paying attention to anything—and she rounded a bend in the path at the bottom of Miller's cow pasture, under a big sycamore tree, and there was a tough-looking boy standing beside a boulder like he was waiting for her.

She stopped short. He stood there ten feet from her, and he wasn't a boy really, he was maybe eighteen years old, and he only had one eye. He wore a black eye patch over the place where his left one should have been, not a spy-movie eye patch but a homemade black-leather flap fastened to a red headband that didn't do a thing to keep his wild black hair in place. Tess saw scars on his face. A wide, stark mouth that did not smile. A single dark, narrow eye staring straight at her.

He stood there with his hands in the pockets of his black jeans like he just happened to be hanging around the creek bottom, but the way he held himself gave him away. His back and shoulders were airy straight, alert and waiting and ready to get him moving in any direction in an instant. Tess knew he was there for a reason.

She didn't smile any more than he did, or say a word—she was frightened. She had heard all the scary stories about what happened to girls who let themselves get caught alone in isolated places. Okay, she was big and strong—that was part of what made her weird, that she was the biggest, strongest girl in school. People might talk behind her back but they'd better not say anything to her face. If this guy tried anything she would fight him, and he was no taller than she was so she figured she had a chance, but—he looked so fierce— what if he had a knife? Tess felt her heart thumping and sweat wetting her palms. She started to back away.

His face didn't change, but he pulled his hands out of his pockets, spreading them empty in the air. "I wouldn't hurt anybody," he said, low-spoken.

Tess didn't necessarily believe what he said, but she liked his voice, gritty and soft. Sounds, their textures and cadences, meant a lot to her. Also, she had enough wrongheaded pride to make her stop backing away and stand still.

He said, "Tessali Rojahin?"

It was her real name, and it scared her worse than anything so far. She blurted out, "No!"

He just stood there with his hands gradually sinking downward, looking at her.

"No. Mathis," she said. "Tess Mathis."

"Okay." He started walking slowly toward her, but she stood still, because he did not seem threatening in the same way any longer. Still dangerous, but in a different way. "Tess. Your stepfather's name is Mathis—"

"He's not my stepfather!" He was her capital-D Daddy. They had never had the money to make it legal, so yes her name was Rojahin on her birth certificate and a few other stupid papers, but as far as Tess was concerned, Benson Mathis was her father.

The stranger boy stood still with his head skewed slightly so that his one eye could watch her. He made her think of a hunting cat, or a sleek black wolf, some sort of wild animal. The way he moved, the way he handled himself, was compact and sure yet shy, the way strong wild animals are shy. "Okay, your adoptive father," he said carefully, sniffing his way, trying to read her. "His name is Mathis."

She stood there without answering.

He said, "But a man named Rojahin—"

"No!" That name panicked her, and this time the fear sent her toward the scar-faced, one-eyed stranger rather than away from him—she just wanted to get past him and get home. She charged him, and he flung up one hand to try to stop her, or maybe to beg her.

"Please," he said, his voice even lower, grainy with what must have been emotion. "Please. I'm trying to find my father."

"Let me alone!" She shoved past him and ran up the pasture hill between rocks and little cedars, which are one of the few things cows won't eat. When she got to the top she had to stop to puff—Appalachian hills will do that to a person. Panting, she looked all around but didn't see anything except a few dirty white cows browsing along the edge of the woods between her and home. She could see in all directions, but the stranger was not in sight. Tess blew her breath out in a sigh, pretty sure that he was not following her.

Pretty sure that he was not trying to hurt her.

Please. I'm trying to find my father.

The hush in his voice, as much as the words themselves, echoed in her mind like a song. There was no Tess Mathis music beating like wings inside her now. Just those words.

But—she couldn't help him, even if she wanted to, because . . . because there was something wrong. With her.

Calm down, Tess told herself, looking out on the shaggy old hills. She tried to remember what Daddy always told her, that she was normal in all the important ways—looks weren't all that important, no matter what certain mall-haired girls thought. So she was oversized and freaky-looking, pink faced, almost pale enough to be an albino, so what. Looks didn't matter and neither did being poor. Tess tried to remember that she was normal in the ways that counted, like having a heart, and knowing good from bad, and worshiping the Phillies during baseball season and the Pittsburgh Steelers the rest of the time. Normal.

Aside from the fact that there was one really strange thing about her: she did not remember anything before she was ten years old.

It was like she didn't have a childhood, because she just didn't remember. Not a thing. Nothing. Blank as a banker's hankie.

2

By the time Tess got home, she had organized her face enough so that she hoped Daddy wouldn't notice anything.

Home was just a cinder-block shack on a slab, like a cow pie with square corners plopped down on the far side of the woods the way people plop little houses sometimes in the country. The clear plastic stretched over the windows for insulation was ripped and made messy noises in the wind. There was more messy ripped plastic stapled over the old wooden screen door on the back, which stuck. When Tess muscled it open and got inside, Daddy was at the stove in his wheelchair, reaching up to stir something in a soup pot.

"Smells good." Tess took the spoon from him, because it's a lot easier for a standing-up person to stir. Daddy seldom complained, but Tess could tell that being in a wheelchair and trying to cook was a pain— Daddy's footrests banged against the stove, and he couldn't see what he was doing. "Yo! Pot pie!" Canned chicken broth with Daddy's hand-rolled homemade noodles swimming around in it, and why it was called pot pie was a mystery, the pie part if not the pot part, but it was yummy. Tess stirred some more, peering hopefully. "No meat?"

"Well, I tell ya, honey, I couldn't quite get Ernestine up to speed to knock off anything." Ernestine was his wheelchair. "Maybe next time I can let 'er rip down Sipe's hill and run over a chipmunk or something."

He was joking. No roadkill was eaten in the Mathis household. At least not yet.

Daddy sighed and said, "I could try Make Money Selling by Phone in Your Spare Time again."

"How would you get the phone put back in?" Tess laid a folded dish towel on the plastic tablecloth and set the pot on it. "Anyway, you made, what, about a penny an hour?" She glanced at him fondly. Daddy had not been a happy telemarketer; he was too nice to talk people into buying junk they didn't want or need. And other than that, there wasn't really much Daddy could do, living way out in the country. Most days he just made his rounds on the roads in his wheelchair. The egg farm put aside cracked eggs for him, and the sexton at the little white shingle-sided crossroads church saved him candle stubs, and old Mrs. Miller next door gave him sugar cookies whenever she baked.

Tess brought a couple of plates from the clutter of dishes sitting on the counter—Daddy couldn't reach things in cupboards—and Daddy wheeled himself up to his place at the table, and the two of them sat and ate. The pot pie was pretty good for something that's really just boiled-up flour held together by an egg and a little Crisco.

"Not bad for an old guy's cooking," Tess teased.

But she knew she'd feel hungry again in half an hour. It wasn't enough to eat. And the food stamps had run out way before the end of the month, as usual. God only knew what there would be to eat tomorrow, especially if Mrs. Miller's lumbago didn't let her get to the kitchen or the chickens forgot to crack some eggs or Ernestine didn't kill a chipmunk.

"Daddy," Tess said, looking down at her empty plate, "school stinks. Really. I'm not learning a thing."

"If you would bring a book home once in a while—"

"It wouldn't make any difference." To Tess, school was just the place where she went to be dumb. "I want to quit. You could say you're home schooling me. I could get a job." *So we can eat,* she was thinking, and Daddy knew it.

"It's not that simple. They got all kinds of requirements for home schooling."

"So we tell them something. Stall them. When I'm sixteen, I can quit."

"You do that, you'll end up regretting it. You drop out, you'll get noplace, end up living in a dump like me."

Tess had heard this before, and it didn't mean a thing to her. Dump? But she liked coming home to this house.

Everything was kind of yellowish, paneling and flowered curtains and secondhand furniture, but what did that matter? Her mother's collectible plates hung on the kitchen wall, Elvis and sad-eyed puppies and cute Amish kids. Tess couldn't remember her mother but she could look at the plates. Her daddy's old stuff, bowling trophies and framed military papers, sat on a shelf in the other room. Her radio was in her bedroom. This was home.

She said, "It's not a dump."

"The heck it's not. Look at me. At my age—"

"It's not your fault you hurt your back."

"I was still going noplace. Busting my ass for the boss man's smart lip and a few dollars. That's why I'm in the fix I'm in, because I got no education. You just stay in school, Tessie. Get your diploma."

The words were worn as smooth as creek stones from being said over and over. They had been said almost every suppertime since the electricity was shut off.

This time, though, suddenly Tess wanted to say new words. *Daddy, there was this stranger down at the bottom of Miller's pasture, asking—*

She felt the watery-awful panic for even thinking it. Always the panic when she thought of asking questions. A few times when she was younger she had asked Daddy about her father or her mother, and his face had gone gray as old chicken bones, and he had given her short answers. Marcus Rojahin was her mother's first husband. Daddy was her mother's second husband. Her

— 9 —

mother was dead. He missed her. And that was it. That was all she knew.

That was all she was going to know, because she'd stopped asking questions. It hurt him too much.

She made herself look at him sitting across from her—just an ordinary going-bald middle-aged guy, aside from the strong arms and shoulders due to wrestling with Ernestine. He had brownish hair turning gray, what was left of it. Brownish eyes flecked with gray like the hair. Extra chin. Extra pounds around the middle from eating dough and eggs instead of decent food. He didn't look a thing like her.

But he was still her Daddy. The one person in the world who cared about her. She would never say a word to him about the stranger boy with his scarred face and his one eye and his black eye patch and his wild black hair. Daddy had enough to worry about.

"Tess." He had noticed her looking at him, and he was smiling back at her. "Hey. You, me, chicken pot pie—it doesn't get any better than this." Making fun of the beer ad.

Suddenly everything was all right. She grinned and started drumming her fingers on the edge of the table.

"All right! It does get better. Give us some music, Tess!"

She grabbed a spoon and got the basic frame going, eight quick steady beats to a bar, on her water glass. Inside the frame her other hand and both her big work-booted feet played around with the twos and fours,

— 10 —

thumping out boogie-rock tempo on the floor, the table, the plastic scrub bucket, the big old tins with cereal boxes crammed into them so ants wouldn't get the corn flakes. Her arms and legs were reaching and pumping and whacking in all directions, her butt started rocking on the chair, and Daddy was bouncing around like she was. There they sat like a pair of nuts, both chair-dancing, Tess and her Daddy.

It didn't get any better than this.

Tess's bed was a studio couch somebody had wanted to get rid of, narrow and lumpy. Usually she lay and let her mind drift until she got comfortable enough to sleep, but that night she went to sleep right away because she didn't want to think.

The next thing she knew she was dreaming about the damn disappearing walls. They were just her bedroom walls, which was what made it so scary, because it was almost as if she were still awake and lying there looking at the Far Side poster Daddy had got her last Christmas and her Def Leppard poster with the one-armed drummer and her endangered species poster from school, but—nothing had happened, yet Tess knew to the marrow of her scared bones that just beyond the faded blue paint the worst thing in the world was on the prowl. It was walled in and it knew her name was Rojahin, it was going to get out and it was going to get her—and then the walls were starting to move. They rippled. They turned thin, like a curtain, and soon she would see the—thing she wasn't supposed to see, she didn't want to see—

She had to wake up, she had to wake up! She woke up.

Then she lay in her bed in the dark thinking *damn*. It had been awhile since she'd had one of her stupid nightmares—why had they started up again? But it didn't matter. Tess knew what to do. She stretched, then settled down with her hands behind her head, reaching for the metal studio couch frame, and she tapped, doing flams and paradiddles, getting a rhythm going. And she hummed along with it. The music started cooking inside her head, and once that happened she was safe. Her music was what kept her sane, kept her from thinking too much about things. About anything.

The next day instead of hiking home from school Tess hiked to the IGA at Hinkles Corner to see if she could get a job. And she lucked out—some woman who wrapped produce had quit in a huff that day. Tess filled out some forms and lied about her age, said she was sixteen, so she could work more hours. She was big enough; they believed her. A woman named Jonna showed her the stockroom and her locker and told her she could start the next day, Saturday.

When she walked out the back door from the stockroom, feeling slightly dazed, there in the gravelly delivery lot stood the stranger boy, headband and homemade eye patch and all, waiting for her by the Dumpster.

Tess wasn't afraid of him this time, just heartily annoyed to see him there because things had been going so well for a minute. She strode up to him. "You've been watching me!" she accused, leaning close to his scarred face. "Following me."

"Only because I have to." His voice stayed soft and low.

"I told you to let me alone."

He lifted his left hand in a kind of appeal, and she noticed something: that hand was stiff and almost useless, as if it had been mangled. "Look, Tess," he said, gently for such a hard-looking person, "I was stupid, I spooked you. Let me explain why I'm here. Please."

She was indeed spooked, but for reasons he didn't know. She knew this Rojahin thing was trouble—she just knew it. Because of the way she couldn't remember. Because of the way Daddy's face went gray. She didn't want to mess with it.

She glared. "I'm late getting home." This was true, and she had a good four-mile hike ahead of her, and from Hinkles Corner it seemed all uphill. The frame houses hung onto hillsides so steep people parked their cars at the bottom, down by the gas station and catalog store and video rental and the IGA. And the rusted railroad line and the creek.

Tess turned uphill and started trudging. But the dark-haired stranger walked along beside her, and when she strode faster so did he.

"Look," he said, "Tess, for starters, I never introduced

myself. My name's Kamo. Kamo Rojahin. Pleased to meet you." He stuck his right hand toward her.

She rolled her eyes, but then she went ahead and shook his hand. Okay, something about him made her think he might not have a permanent address, but it wasn't like he smelled bad. His hair had a shine to it, even though it looked wild as a black pony's mane in the wind. His clothes were nice enough—plain jeans, plain faded-blue pocket tee, cleaner than hers. He didn't look like he had head lice or fleas. But Tess made her handshake quick and halfhearted and kept walking.

"I'm looking for my father," he said, businesslike, "and I'm here because your name's Rojahin, like mine."

How did he know? He must have tracked her down through courthouse papers. "It's not," she said. "It's just the name on my birth certificate."

"Okay. But you got to admit it's not a real common name. I'm wondering if we're related some way."

She stopped walking and turned to face him. Hinkles Corner was not exactly a metropolis, and they had reached the edge of it. Tess was ready to turn off the road and cut across country, and she didn't want to walk any farther with this Kamo Rojahin person by her side. What the hell kind of name was Kamo anyway? And who the hell was he? He didn't look a thing like her. She was as pale as a person can get, and he was dark. She could have played fullback for Penn State, and he was slim and lithe. He was crazy if he thought they were related.

Although—there was something alike about the shape of their faces. Straight brows. Square jaws. Chins that meant business. And something—Tess couldn't quite say what—some glimmer in his one good eye that reminded her of a shadow she had sometimes seen in her own mirror.

"Where are you from?" Tess demanded.

He looked back at her quietly with the old stony hills rising behind him and the low evening light flashing off his black hair and battered face. "Nowhere. I mean, lots of places."

Was he a runaway or something? A fugitive? A criminal?

Tess couldn't place him. He seemed too old to be as young as he looked, and he seemed like a drifter yet something about him felt solid, and she couldn't get past the way he talked, though she couldn't have explained what it was about the way he talked that stopped her. Hard-voiced, she said, "How do I know your name's what you say it is? How do I know you're not some kind of con artist?"

Kamo took a minute to answer, thinking, though his scarred face did not move. "You don't," he said finally. "You don't know a thing about me."

She gave him a look that expressed her opinion, and maybe he got the message, because when she walked away he stood by the road and watched her go.

3

Tess went to her first day of work not expecting much except a paycheck. Certainly not expecting her heart to turn inside out.

Then she heard "Secret Star."

She hadn't dared to hope there would be real radio. In the front of the store where the customers were they played watered-down music like in the dentist's office. But in the back, where Tess was, in the stockroom—radio. Real radio, classic rock and the latest hits—for Tess it was as if she'd been reunited with a best friend, with a long-lost brother, with the mother who used to sing her to sleep at night. Her heart felt hot. They were playing mostly standard music, stuff she already knew, but now she listened in a trance. Barely heard people talking as she wrapped radishes. It had been so long—

When the first steel-blue guitar notes rang out, she forgot all about radishes and stood with the price gun in her hand pointing toward the sky. Then the singer's voice made her gasp. A voice of flint and moonlight. It began deep in his chest and rose like a hawk on the wind as Tess stood listening with her mouth hanging open, barely breathing.

> *In the sin-bin city*
> *you can't see far*
> *In the shadows*
> *the bad pose*
> *bullets fly*
> *sirens cry*
> *the blood flows*
> *blows stun*
> *children sob for pity*
> *children cry for pity—*
> *But out past the pollution*
> *out beyond the fear*
> *out beyond the shadows*
> *shines a secret star*

It was kind of like poetry, because the words mattered, they drove the song. But it wasn't just the words, because this dude could sing—oh, Mama, could he sing, with grit and gut but never just screaming out the lyrics—there was pain, but he got beyond it and turned it into real music. His whole sound was stony real. He was by himself, no band, no fake violins in the background, not even a drum machine—it was naked, the way he used his guitar for percussion, and Tess the drummer felt chills just listening. Among all the slick synthesized oh-baby-baby let's-have-sex garbage on the top 40, this guy stood out like a lonesome bright star in a black-plastic sky.

"Who is that?" Tess blurted out.

The white-coated people in the back of the IGA looked at her.

"Singing! On the radio!" she yelled as if they were the ones acting weird. "Who is it?"

"Where you been, in a cave?" asked a high-school boy working across from her.

"Nobody knows," said the woman who ran the stock-room.

"Huh?"

"Nobody knows."

"It's a big honkin' hairy mystery," the boy said.

The woman said, "He's the secret star."

And the song hawk-swooped on, crying straight to Tess's heart:

> *In this dirty world*
> *you can't see far*
> *but you gotta believe*
> *there's a secret star. . .*

Tess had not been in a cave, just home with no electricity, no radio—but she had heard kids in school talking about some secret star thing. Hadn't paid any attention. Just another fad, like designer jeans or the latest fashion model. If they liked it, she wouldn't.

In a way she had been wrong. And in a way she had

been right. The other kids liked it, but she had been struck by lightning, she was riding a golden eagle, she was falling into a great white light. She stood listening to the last few bars as if she were tuned in to angels on high, and the boy across the table from her stood watching her. He grinned. "All the girls are hot for the secret star." Teasing.

"He don't call himself that," said the stockroom woman. "He don't mean the song that way." She was middle-aged and sad-eyed and she seemed to understand. "It's the deejays call him that."

Sure enough, the deejay was yammering. "Waaal, paint me green and call me Gumby! Six weeks at number one and no concerts, no video, no pretty face, and that's about as alternative as it comes—it's not supposed to be able to be done, dudes! Hey, didja hear the latest rumor? This guy is supposed to be a captain in the Marines, that's why he won't come forward, he's afraid they'll think he's gay. Ha-ha! Hey, do you believe that? I don't believe that. I like the one where he's supposed to be Jim Morrison's ghost. Whoo—ee! Keep it right here, people. Coming up—"

Tess stopped listening. She tuned out. Didn't want anything to steal the sound of that song from her mind.

"He calls himself Crux," the gentle-eyed woman said. Tess looked blank, so she said it again. "The secret star calls himself Crux."

"It's a gimmick," said the boy, slapping paper tape around bunches of bananas. Tess knew who he was

— 19 —

from school; everybody knew who he was. His name was Butch. He was an athlete, good-looking, with muscles and a cute grin. He was one of the popular boys. Tess had never spoken to him, because why would he want to talk to her? She wasn't cute. No boy would ever like her. But here he was talking to her about "Secret Star."

He said, "It's hype. Take a stupid song, make a big mystery out of it, and people go crazy, and somebody's raking in a pile of money."

He didn't understand. That was okay; Tess didn't expect everybody to understand about "Secret Star." How could they? It was a mystery song, a miracle song, a fusion of rap and rock and a throwback to folk at the same time, all melted together with a little bit of country and so much soul it made her want to dance naked in the rain, which was pretty radical considering that she didn't know how to dance and she hated rain. Hype? No. What Tess heard was stone-bone real music, the kind only a real musician can deliver. Whatever was making this singer hide behind his song had nothing to do with making a pile of money. Tess didn't know how to say this to Butch, but she knew it for a fact, like knowing the sky is high.

Kamo knocked during supper. Tess looked up and saw who was standing outside and made her face freeze to show nothing. "Come in," Daddy called without even looking up, but Kamo didn't come in. He stood outside and spoke through the ripped plastic that was supposed to be covering the screen door, talking straight to Daddy.

"You got work I can do? For food?"

Food was something the Mathis household actually had now, because Tess's boss, Jonna, had sent her home loaded down with two-day-old bread, dented cans of beans, damaged freezer boxes of meat. "Kindness of strangers," Daddy had said. "How did she know?" Though probably Jonna had seen the Mathises spend their food stamps at the IGA often enough. Anyway, there was no place to keep the frozen stuff with the fridge not running, so they had cooked several packets of meat all at once—the stove ran on bottle gas, thank God. Processed beef patties in gravy sat steaming on the table. There was hot cooked food on a chilly April day, and there was plenty for Kamo.

Daddy told him, "Come in here where I can see you, son."

Kamo slipped in and stood on the cracked linoleum just inside the door, looking at Daddy, not looking at Tess. *Smart boy,* she thought. One look, one smirk, and she would have considered putting her table knife into him like he was butter for her bread. *Smart boy, you'd better keep quiet.* He had been spying on her again, and probably this "work for food" thing was a trick to get into her house. She sat glaring at him, but she couldn't say anything in front of Daddy. Probably Kamo was counting on that.

Well, he could count on this, too: he'd better not do or say anything to make Daddy upset.

"What's your name?" Daddy asked him.

"Kamo."

Daddy lifted his eyebrows, waiting for the rest of it.

"Just Kamo. Or Kam."

Tess breathed out. Kamo hadn't told Daddy "Rojahin." He hadn't smirked, either. She started to simmer down.

"Huh." Daddy nodded as if he now knew enough. "Kam, why don't you wash your hands. We don't have no spigot water right now, but there's a pump in the yard. Soap's on the trough. Then c'mon in and have a seat and join us."

The thing about Daddy, Tess thought, was that for a guy in a wheelchair he had a lot of pride. Not stuck-up pride, but the kind of pride that made him put something in the "Help a Child" can on the drugstore counter even though his disability check barely paid the mortgage. The kind that made him stay in his own house in the country even though he could have gone on welfare and moved to some sort of subsidized apartment in town where the food pantries and public transportation and stuff were. The kind that made him offer a meal to a scar-faced loner he ought to be afraid of.

Kamo had pride, too. Before he moved to do what Daddy said he asked, "You got work I can do?"

"Later, son. You can't work when you're hungry."

Kam really was hungry. Ravenous. He seemed wobbly as he sat down at the table. His hands shook when he reached for the spoon to ladle some meat and gravy on his bread.

Nobody talked much. Kamo was busy gulping, and Tess was watching him narrow-eyed, and Daddy was thinking about what he wanted him to do. Tess could see him thinking. "Slice of jelly bread?" he asked when Kam's plate was empty, even though Kam had already had three slices of bread to sop up his gravy.

"I think I better quit before I get a gut ache." Kam turned his head so he could look at Daddy with his one eye, and the look was his thanks.

Daddy nodded. "You still got a couple of hours of daylight left," he said. "You think if Tess helps you find the ladder you could get up on the roof and clean the gutters and check the shingles?"

"Daddy," Tess complained, "I could do that myself." Why did he have to act like she was a little girl? She could do things. She just hadn't thought about cleaning the stupid gutters.

"Not when it's just me around. What if you fell? I couldn't help you."

"I wouldn't fall!"

Kam was on his feet as if he were giving the Mathises room to argue, clearing his dishes off the table, taking them to the sink. He turned on a spigot to rinse his plate, and nothing came out. All Tess could see was the eye-patch side of his face, and it didn't move, yet she got the feeling he was flustered. He put his plate down and turned the spigot off.

Daddy was saying to her, "You don't know what might happen. Look at me. Crap can happen anytime."

Tess always felt like shaking Daddy when he said "Look at me"—it was so preachy. She wanted to argue more, but Kam was on his way out the door, and she got up and headed after him. Once the two of them got to the shed and out of earshot of the house, she said to him none too politely, "What are you doing here?"

"I was hungry." He was already getting the ladder down from the shed rafters, but he let one end of it bang to the dirt floor and turned on Tess. "Why don't you want me here?" His voice was soft and fierce. "What kind of person do you think I am?"

She stared at him. It was dark in the shed. She couldn't see his single eye. Her chest hurt, but not with fear. Why wasn't she afraid?

He said, "It's like in the old movies, is that it? The ones with the messed-up faces, the hacked-off noses or whatever, those are the bad guys. You think I'm a bad guy, right?"

She didn't watch old movies much, or any movies, but she knew what he meant. She knew it all too well, and didn't answer.

He made a small, disgusted noise through his nose, took the ladder and strode out of the shed.

4

Tess watched Kam set the ladder up against the house. With quick, edgy movements he climbed to the roof and started working on the gutters, scraping last year's rotting leaves out of them with his hands.

Tess hit her fist quietly against the shed door for a moment, then went back into the shed and found a couple of trowels and an old peach basket. Carrying the tools, she climbed the ladder and walked along the edge of the roof to where Kam was working.

"Here," she said, poking a trowel toward him.

He jumped so hard it startled her heart like a grouse going up. He leaped to his feet and jerked around to face her, coiling as if she had come at him with a switch-blade, his single eye white-rimmed like the huge eye of a spooked horse—and his right foot missed the edge of the roof. It caught on the gutter a moment but the gutter started to let go and all of a sudden the idea of falling off the roof was no joke—Tess saw Kam's mouth open as he lost balance and wavered at the edge, though he didn't scream.

Tess never remembered grabbing, but the next heartbeat she had hold of him by both arms, trowels and peach basket were clattering down but he was okay, standing on the roof, back from the edge. She could feel him trembling.

"Jesus," he panted, "you blindsided me!" He had been concentrating on what he was doing, or maybe on being mad at her, and she had come up to him on his eyepatch side. He had not known she was there.

"Sorry!" she said at the same time. "I'm sorry." She meant sorry for everything, because it was true, what he had said in the shed. She had been making assumptions about him. "You okay?"

"Yeah." He muttered it—now he was embarrassed. He pulled away from her and turned back to what he had been doing, hunkering down by the gutter again, straightening the bent place with his hands—mostly with his right hand, because his left hand wasn't worth much. "Thanks," he said without looking at her.

She retrieved the trowels and peach basket, took a trowel, and went to the other end of the gutter from him and started cleaning it out. There was so much dirt in there that little maple trees had taken root, each of them just a sprout and one leaf—they reminded Tess of eighth notes sprouting up from the top of a music staff, except their baby leaves looked glassy and almost pink in the evening light. She tossed them and rotting gutter trash into the peach basket, which she had put halfway between her and Kam, and as she worked she moved slowly toward him.

Something about the low light and sunset glow felt like French-horn music—it made Tess calm down, and she got a gentle rhythm going in her head, and she did some pretty clear thinking. About Kam. She still didn't know a thing about him, and she got the feeling he wasn't going to tell her much. He wanted her to trust him. And she wasn't sure she should, because it looked like he had been a gang fighter, or at least he had spent a lot of time on rough streets. Why else would he react that way when a person took him by surprise? And all the scars—if he had been a gang fighter, that would explain how he had gotten them. And if he had been in a gang, why should she trust him?

Yet, Tess knew, she did trust him. She trusted him to understand.

In the shed, she had known to her bones that he would not hurt her.

More than that. She trusted him more than that.

Across the little distance that still separated them she called to him, "Have you heard a song called 'Secret Star'?"

His head came up, and he turned toward her so he could look at her, though the look didn't tell her whether he knew what she was talking about.

"I am in love with that song," she told him.

He smiled. It was the first time she had seen him smile, and it was a wide, warm, million-dollar smile that lit up his one-eyed face and made her forget the scars.

"I just heard it for the first time today," she said. "I am going crazy. That song gives me chills and fever. I need to get a radio. I need to get the CD. I need to get a CD player." Yeah, right, and a pig with wings. "I want to put that song under my pillow." Somehow she needed to have it to keep. All her life she would love it.

For some reason, maybe because he was actually smiling, Kam ducked his head and turned back to his work.

The peach basket was getting in the way. Tess shoved it back with her foot. She and Kam worked shoulder to shoulder digging out the last three feet of gutter, comfortable together, neither of them speaking.

The singer, Tess wondered briefly, the secret star— who was he? But no, she didn't really want to know. It would break her heart if he turned out to be what Butch had said, some plastic Hollywood guy using mystery as a sales gimmick. Forget about him. He was a star, and people like that, stars, they lived at the opposite end of the universe from real people like her. Stars never set foot on Appalachian hills, never stepped in cow poop, never—probably never talked to homely girls like her. Tess didn't want to know who he was, because this way she could pretend his song was speaking straight to her.

The song was the important thing; it meant something. Like, there was a star out beyond everything, like, there was hope, there was light—that was what mattered. The singer didn't matter as much as the song.

Yet when Tess went to bed that night and lay there with the song fever pulsing in her, not even trying to go to sleep, she daydreamed about him. The singer. In her mind she gave him form, and he was a passionate angel of a man, more beautiful than any man she had ever met, with his heartbeat drumming in his temples and his long hair lifting like a stallion's mane and a face worth weeping over and under his perfect brows his hot eyes shining like a thousand stars.

The next day, Sunday, Tess's day off, Kamo came back to the Mathis place to help clean the cistern.

Benson Mathis had told Kamo he was welcome to sleep in the shed, but Kam said he had a place to sleep. He showed up in time for breakfast, and then except for lunch he and Tess worked all day. Tess found him good to work with—steady, quiet, didn't talk constantly or get peevish about little things or sling orders around, which was more than she could say for some people at the IGA. She found it hard to stay on guard against him.

Cleaning the cistern was a bear of a job. It took both of them to heave the cover off, and then they had to get all the water out with buckets on ropes, and then they had to get into the cistern, which if you are not real fond of dark, cramped, damp places is like crawling into hell. Then they had to scrape out all the gunk that had come down from the gutters, and scour slime off the bottom and sides, then rinse the cistern out with water hauled from the hand pump in the backyard. Then they dipped out the dirty rinse water because they couldn't just run it off through the spigots because the electric pump wasn't working. And cleaning the cistern while it wasn't being used had sounded like such a good idea.

"You got any more torture for us?" Tess asked Daddy when she and Kamo were finished with the stinking cistern.

"Sure. I got a list long as my arm."

She and Kamo went around and ripped the ratty plastic off the doors and windows. Then they cleaned out the accumulation of winter trash in the shed. Then they went up on the roof and admired their clean gutters and looked for loose shingles and nailed on some new ones. All that time Kam didn't ask about Tess's Rojahin father, and she sensed that he was not going to, not when they were working. So as far as she was concerned they could just keep working, and they did, right until dark. When Daddy finally called them in for supper, she was so tired she felt silly.

Daddy had creamy beeswax candles from the crossroads church stuck in mayo-jar lids for light. "No dessert," he said cheerfully after the Mathises and guest had devoured half a loaf of bread and a big box of fish sticks. Daddy was in a happy mood. "No sorbet, and no strolling violinists either, but who needs 'em? Give us some music, Tess!"

In front of Kamo? But why not. The rebel in Tess tried never to care what other people thought. She put the flats of her fingers on the table and started drumming.

In her head she had been working out a rhythm arrangement for "Secret Star," and it had been simmering and stewing and brewing in her all day, and when she started drumming it was like starting a nuclear reaction. Fusion. She leaned into a light-speed double-stroke roll and kicked out for things to bang with both feet, she was slapping out eighths with one hand and triplets with the other, popping snare chops against a table leg, drumming till her chair shook, every muscle rocking. Kam looked stunned. In the candlelight his eye shone as big as a half-dollar, and who could blame him.

Daddy was laughing. "Groove it, Tess!"

Suddenly she felt like a clown and discovered that she did care what Kam thought after all. Hot-faced, she stopped.

"Keep going!" Kam exclaimed, but she shook her head.

"You take drum lessons?" He leaned over the table toward her.

"A little," she mumbled. "In school."

"You drummed for bands?"

She shook her head, got up and headed out to the black backyard where there was more work waiting.

Benson Mathis sat in his wheelchair and watched as Kam got up and followed Tess out the door. Benson Mathis sighed.

Tess has a secret.

The way she and this Kamo guy accepted each other without talking made him feel like they had met before Kam came to the house, like Kam might be hanging around for reasons other than work and food. Not surprising. Tess was one heck of a good-looking girl. Didn't think it of herself, but she was. Big and strong and gorgeous, like a cream-colored '59 Cadillac Eldorado. Of course, he was biased. His daughter—stepdaughter—wasn't just the main thing that kept him going; she was the only thing. All he had left of the woman who had been the love of his life.

And pretty soon, just like her mother had done, Tess was going to leave him. Not for some guy, necessarily, but one way or another she was going to leave. Look at the way she had gone and got herself that job.

She's growing up.

This Kamo guy, now, he was too old for her. Too old and been around too much. That didn't bother Benson Mathis, because he knew himself to be a good judge of character and he pegged Kam as what they used to call a "gentleman." Dangerous, maybe, but not to Tess. Had hurt some people, maybe, but would never take advantage of a girl.

Benson Mathis recognized "gentleman" in Kamo because he strove for that same quality in himself. Do the right thing. Protect women and children. Raise the little girl to grow up sweet and strong.

Pretty soon I'm gonna have to let her go.

Still—in a few minutes he would call her in from the yard. Yeah, she had to grow up, but nobody could blame him for trying to put it off as long as he could.

He relaxed in his wheelchair, closed his eyes, and sighed again.

I'm a coward.

Putting things off was one way of hoping they never had to happen. Though he was not consciously thinking of it, in the back of Benson Mathis's mind there was a shadow. Always there whenever he thought about Tess. The reason he had never taken her to experts to have her memory loss treated. He wanted to put off the day she might remember. He hoped she would never remember. If she did, she might leave him that minute and never come back.

Tess struggled with the heavy, wet clothing she had put in a tub of soapy water to soak. It was difficult to rinse it thoroughly and hang it up in the dark.

Kamo had followed her out to the pump. "You know rhythms they never taught you in school," he said.

"Huh," Tess grunted, tipping the heavy washtub. So

she'd played along with the radio a lot, big deal. A heck of a lot of good knowing drum rhythms would ever do her. No way could she make a living playing drums, that was what Daddy said and so did everybody else. A person had to do something practical to get by in this world. Anyway, bands didn't want girl drummers, not if they were guy bands, which they mostly were.

Kam took one side of the washtub and helped her heave it under the pump, then started pumping. "You planning on going into music?" he called to her above the squeaking of the handle.

"Not really."

"You're *not?*" His voice went high, but then he tried to soften it. "You got other plans?"

Tess shrugged.

"You crazy, Tess?" She could barely see his face, but she could hear the fervor in his voice. "God, girl, you want to waste your life? You need to go into music. You're talented."

Tess had never much liked being told what she "needed" to do. "I know people who can twirl a baton with their toes. It's just about as useful."

"This is different. My God, you were playing eight-thirteen time in there. And you've only had a few lessons? You must have a music gene the size of Milwaukee."

"You can stop pumping." She tipped out the rinse water, grunting and thinking sour thoughts: So how did Kamo Rojahin come to be an authority on eight-

— 34 —

thirteen time and music genes? She straightened up to look at him. "You went to Juilliard or something?" she asked him, sarcastic.

There was a silence. Then, "My father was a musician," he said, his voice so low she could barely hear him.

Oh, God. Instantly she felt awful. But at the same time she felt terrified.

"Tess, listen—"

She turned away from him and started snatching soggy clothes out of the washtub and slinging them at the clothesline as fast as she could for a person who could not see what she was doing.

"Could you just tell me what your father looked like?"

"No."

"You might be my sister, or my cousin." He kept his voice very low; Daddy wouldn't hear. "Don't you care?" The words quavered. He tried to lighten up. "One way or another?"

She had only known him a couple of days, and she was still half afraid of him, but yes, damn it, she did care. She cared unbelievably.

She stood there with a pair of Daddy's pull-on sweatpants dripping on her feet, and Kamo stood there with his bent hand lifted toward her, waiting for an answer. And she gave it to him by telling him the truth. "I can't remember."

"Huh?" His hand sank slowly down.

"I can't remember my father."

"You can't remember?" He spoke slowly, as if unsure of her. "You were too young?"

"No. I mean, I don't think so. I—I just can't remember." She turned to him even though he was only a shape in the dark. "I'm—there's something wrong with me."

She told him about it, and he stood listening—it was easier to talk to him when she couldn't see his scarred face. Or maybe she had been needing to talk to someone—but it wasn't as if she could have told just anybody. There was something about Kamo. She blurted it all out, how she didn't remember her father or mother at all and Daddy was no help, how her life had seemingly started when she was ten, how she blanked out when she tried to go back any farther.

"You don't remember your first day of school?"

"Nope."

"Your birthday parties?"

"No. Nothing."

"Good Lord, Tess." He sounded uncertain. "Does it bother you?"

"Kind of, yeah, but kind of no. Not really." It wasn't like a person had to remember kindergarten or birthday parties to get a job or do any of the practical things. Okay, she hated her nightmares—but other people had nightmares too, right? There might not even be a connection.

Right.

Almost plaintively Kamo asked, "Don't you ever wonder? Don't you want family?"

"I've got Daddy."

Kamo stood silent. Tess grew afraid.

"Kam—don't say anything to him."

Kam swiveled his head as if he were looking at her, though he couldn't see her face in the dark. "He never told you anything?"

"A little. It bothers him when I ask. Kam, please, don't go asking him stuff."

The back door opened, and there was Daddy, as if somebody had called his name. Against the puny candlelight Tess could see his silhouette as he wheeled his chair so he could look out the screen door. "Tess?" he hollered. She and Kamo had been out there a pretty long time.

"Just a minute!" she hollered back.

She got the feeling he thought she and Kamo were doing some kind of boy-girl thing but he didn't want to say it. "Clothes giving you fits?" he yelled.

"Yeah, they're all tangled up." She rushed to sling the rest of them on the line. Kam came over and helped.

"How'd he hurt his back?" he asked in a very low voice as the two of them bent over the washtub together.

"He doesn't want to talk about that either. He was a bulldozer operator. Some sort of accident."

Kam was silent.

"Kam," she begged, "please promise me you won't hassle him."

"I keep telling you, I wouldn't do anything to hurt anybody." Kam draped the last undershirt over the clothesline, turned the tub upside down to drain, and straightened up to face Tess. "Did he ever tell you your father's first name?"

"Sure." It was on her birth certificate, so she had to know it. "Marcus. Marcus Rojahin."

Kamo nodded, as if he knew all along. "My father's name was Marco."

Tess stood stunned. Marco, Marcus, and the same weird last name—could they be the same person? Up until that moment she had not truly believed it could be happening. "Oh, my God," she whispered.

"So you see why I'm here," he said, and he walked off into the night.

"You want some of this Pepsi?" Butch asked Tess.

"Sure." Of course she wanted some. She wanted a soda of her own, but she couldn't have it, and she hated that. Whenever she was in the IGA she had to look at aisles and aisles of things she couldn't have, not when there were so many things she and Daddy needed worse. Whenever she went on break she craved the dumb things most people could buy without a second thought: pretty cards in the card aisle, shiny heart-shaped balloons, bunches of flowers. Donuts. Bright markers. Snickers bars. Pepsi.

I hate being poor.

"You don't mind drinking out of the same can, do you?" Butch passed it to her without waiting for an answer. Yes, she did kind of mind, but she drank anyway.

They were both sweeping up. Grapes made the worst mess, loose ones rolling under the tables and squished ones and shredded leaves and squiggly bits of stem. Tess muscled her big push broom and drank Pepsi at the same time. "You're in ninth grade, right?" Butch asked.

"Right." She smiled at him. Probably he was just being nice, but still, it felt good. She never would have dreamed that a good-looking, popular boy like Butch would act interested in her, even if it was just because he worked with her.

In the same easy tone he asked, "How old are you?"

"Fourteen."

"So how come they're letting you work here?"

Too late Tess saw her mistake. "No. Sixteen," she said. "I meant sixteen. I'm in ninth grade but I'm sixteen." She was talking too fast and her voice wanted to rise. "They held me back. I flunked a couple of grades in elementary school."

He had stopped sweeping and stood watching her with that cocky grin of his. "Bull," he said.

"Butch." She managed to keep her voice down, almost whispering; what if Lupe heard, or Jonna? "Please. I need this job. Don't tell."

"You bad girl." He was smiling, teasing. "You lied. What if I tell?"

"Butch, *please.*"

"Relax, Tess." He smiled a different way and turned back to his sweeping. "How old are you? Sixteen, right?"

"Right." Her voice was creaky, her knees shaky with relief. "Thanks." He was nice after all. Just for a second there she had felt like he wasn't.

"No problem," he said. "Sometime you'll do something for me."

When she got out of work Tess looked for Kam. She walked all around the building. He wasn't there.

She hadn't seen him for a couple of days. Each night when she walked out the IGA's back door she was looking for him, but he wasn't there. All the way up the steep road out of Hinkles Corner and cutting through the salvage yard and down a dirt track past the sawmill and along a tractor path and the creek path and through the rocks and up Miller's pasture, all the way home she was looking for him, but he wasn't there. And she didn't know where he was staying. Sleeping in somebody's barn, probably, God knew where. There was no good reason for her to be looking for him—it would have been just too bizarre to really think he was her brother—but he was on her mind like the "Secret Star" song. She flunked two quizzes in school those couple of days, and when she thought of Kam her chest felt so hollow she didn't care.

Wednesday at work she was flattening empty cardboard boxes, and she had heard "Secret Star" twice and knew she would never in her life get tired of it, when the sweet-faced, sad-eyed woman, Lupe, came back from break and said to her, "There's a boy waiting out back to see you when you get a chance."

Tess's head jerked up so quickly her neck cracked.

"If it's that ugly-faced one-eyed friend of yours," Butch said, "tell him to bug off."

How the—how did he know about Kam? She gawked at him.

"He's been hanging around, asking questions," Butch said. "Tell him to stay out of my face." He patted his pocket as if that was supposed to mean something, turned and swaggered away. He often swaggered, but he couldn't help that; he was a jock. Was he mad? Tess stared after him.

"He tries to be a big man so his father will notice him," Lupe said.

Butch's father was some sort of Army general stationed at the base in the mountains outside of Canadawa, where Tess went to school. Butch mentioned his father a lot. His father was away at the Pentagon, his father had to go to a meeting with the secretary of state, that sort of thing.

"Huh," Tess said, and she went on break.

The boy waiting out back was Kamo.

Kam didn't lean against the Dumpster—he stood straight and still, waiting beside it. "Hey," he said, friendly but unsmiling, as Tess walked up to him.

"Kam, this guy I work with says you've been asking questions."

He acknowledged with a nod. "I was hoping other people around here might know your father."

"Oh, great. Just wonderful." She was glad to see him,

yet suddenly she was angry at him. "Talking about me behind my back."

"Not about you."

"About my father, same thing."

Kam said, with passion yet without raising his voice, "What else am I supposed to do? I need to find him. You can't help me."

Damn, he was right. There was nothing else he could do except go away, and she didn't want that. She let out a long breath and said nothing.

"Anyway, no such luck," Kam said more quietly. "It seems like you and Mr. Mathis are kind of new here. Just moved here four, five years ago. Nobody knows a thing."

"Huh!" Tess was taken aback. Somehow she had assumed that she and Daddy had lived in the little cow-plop cinder-block shack in the country since she was born. But it seemed not.

It seemed like Daddy had let her think that, though.

Kam gave her a minute to process the information, and then he asked, "Tess—why don't you remember?"

Dumb question. "I just don't."

"Because you're a mental deficient? I don't think so. Tess, c'mon. Why?"

No, it wasn't such a dumb question. Something dark and hard had started to gather in her chest and she didn't have a name for it but she knew it was the bomb that was going to blow the walls of her world in. She admitted it, though only to herself: some horrible thing had happened when she was a child, something so awful she could not remember.

Kam said, "Don't you want to know about your parents? Aren't you curious?"

She shook her head vehemently.

"Tess," he said, "I'm asking your permission to talk to Mr. Mathis."

She knew he was. "Go away."

He could tell she didn't mean it. He turned to go, but said gently, "I'll be back when you get off work."

How he knew when she got off work was a mystery to Tess, because she had never told him. Maybe he just stood there for hours. When she came out, though, there he was by the Dumpster, swiveling his head to check her face like a hawk checking to see which way the wind was blowing. She didn't know what to say to him, but stood and waited for him to come and walk beside her before she headed toward home.

Neither of them said a word as they walked up Hinkles Corner. Tess trudged more slowly than usual, noticing things, as if that could help her. Outhouses. Somebody had a plywood cutout, a granny fanny, leaning against an outhouse. Springtime, so people were putting ornaments on their lawns, propeller-wing ducks, kissing kids, plastic pinwheel daisies. Some old woman even had the push mower out already. Tess saw yellow posy bushes blooming, yellow smoke rising from a chimney—somebody had a coal fire going. It was going to be a chilly night.

She and Kam said nothing until they were clear out of Hinkles Corner, through the salvage yard and past the sawmill and into river-bottom country. It was dusk by then, with the evening star coming out like a highlight in a polished brass sky. There was light enough for Tess to see Kamo's scarred face when she turned to him.

"Okay," she said to him, hard. "You want to find your father."

He nodded.

"Why?" she demanded. He'd better have a good answer to justify what he was putting her through, not some selfish reason. Heck, for all she knew he might want a place where he could stay and not have to work. He might want to tell his father off. He might want to kill him.

"That's kind of a dumb question," Kam said.

"No, it's not. No dumber than a lot of the questions you're asking me. Why is it so important to find your father?"

He stopped walking, but he didn't answer right away. He stood where he was and looked off to where the dark hills crowded against the golden-bugle color in the sky. On the nearest hillside an old orchard hulked, overgrown with poison ivy. Everywhere the stony farms were abandoned, pastures going to locust and cedar, wilderness taking them back.

Night noises were starting. Spring frogs.

Kam said, so softly she could barely hear him, "You'll think I'm a jerk."

"Maybe." She could not afford to have mercy. Her voice came out as hard as the stony hills. "What do you want your father for?"

He took a breath and looked straight at her with his head lifted, defiant, as he said it. "Love."

Tess gawked at him.

"I want somebody to love me," he said, and his voice didn't stay quite steady, and neither did his face.

It took her breath away. No boy she knew or had ever known would have had the guts to say it, to tell the real reason. Boys she knew at school, trying so hard to be cool in hundred-dollar running shoes—they would have joked around. Or they would have come out with some lame reason, like wanting money. Or they would have gotten all studly and mad.

Kam wasn't being macho. Just for that alone the whole world should have loved him.

"You don't—have anybody?"

He shook his head. His face flinched, and he turned away.

They walked on, and Tess knew what she had to do, both for him and for herself. But it was dark, with the stars shining up from the black creek water, before she could say it.

"Okay," she told Kam. "Talk to Daddy."

When Tess walked in she saw dinner waiting on the table and Daddy waiting to eat with her. "Kamo," he said, looking a little surprised and not quite happy when

Kam walked in with her. Tess saw him trying not to jump to conclusions. Daddy was fair. "You looking for supper again?" he asked, making himself smile at Kam. Daddy had manners. "Put on another plate, Tess."

Kam shook his head. "No," he said, his voice low, "I didn't come for supper." Tess knew he wasn't about to eat Daddy's macaroni and cheese when he planned on asking unwelcome questions. He leaned against the sink edge, bracing himself. From his wheelchair Daddy peered up at him.

"What's wrong, son?"

"Mr. Mathis, I need to talk with you."

But then Kam didn't seem to know what to say, and Tess saw the color start to seep out of Daddy's face, saw him going gray, saw his hands clutch at Ernestine's wheels. "Daddy," she said, butting in to get this over with, "Kam's last name is Rojahin. He's looking for his father. He thinks maybe—"

"No," Daddy said sharply.

"I haven't seen him since I was a little kid," Kam said. "I don't know where to start."

"Not here." Daddy's hands jerked backward, rolling his chair away from Kam till it bumped against the table; the lid slid off the macaroni pan with a crash. "I don't want—"

"Mr. Mathis, please. Just tell me where—"

"No!" The color rushed back to Daddy's face, and he heaved himself up in his chair and roared. "You back off! I don't want you bothering Tess with this nonsense."

She had hardly ever in her life sided against him, but this was one time. "Daddy," she told him, "I need to know too."

"No, you don't!" He swung his chair toward her almost like a threat. "No, you don't, Tess!"

"Just tell me where you lived before you came here," Kam said, keeping the volume down. "Tell me where I might find him, that's all."

"I'm telling you nothing! Nothing!" Daddy reared forward in his wheelchair, his face so flushed even his bald spot was red. "You get out of here!"

Kamo swallowed hard, gripped the edge of the sink and didn't move.

"Get out and stay out! I don't want you bothering my daughter."

Tess was getting frightened. Not that Daddy would hurt anybody, even though he was yelling—*Why should it scare me?* But it did.

"Get out of here! Now!"

It was like—an echo, a voice she had heard before, roaring—in a nightmare that turned walls to tissue. Tess stood with the kitchen floor solidly under her big feet, and she knew every splotch on the linoleum, and the grease-freckled walls were not really billowing like sheets in a high wind, but—they had been—somewhere—

"This is my house! Get out of my house!"

There had been another house—not like this one, all one flat cluttered story without any steps even at the

— 48 —

front and back doors, but a—a house with stairs, a big house where a half-grown girl had crouched on the tall stairs and peeked down through the white spindle railing—

"Get—out—"

Daddy's shouting turned to gasping. His face turned from red to putty pale, and he sank down in his chair. Tess could see him sweating. Could see how his hands shook as they clutched at Ernestine's wheels.

"Daddy!" She got herself moving and hurried toward him.

"My pills," he whispered, and then he yelled it, his voice hoarse. "Tess, get my pills!"

His heart medicine—it had to be on the junked-up kitchen counter somewhere, but she couldn't think where. She sent dishes clattering, trying to find it. Kam turned to help.

"Go away," she snapped, panicked and angry—at him, at herself, for asking stupid questions that could kill Daddy, give him a heart attack. "Do what he says, get out!"

She didn't look, just heard the door close as Kamo left.

"Okay, Daddy." At last she found the pills and got the bottle open. She gave him two. "Just relax." She dipped him a glass of drinking water from the covered bucket that sat by the sink. After the pills took effect and Daddy's breathing quieted down and his shaking stopped and his color was better, he just sat in his chair.

Slack, like he'd been beaten up. Tess would have french-fried herself sooner than ask him any more questions. She offered to heat up supper but he didn't want any. He said he wasn't hungry. Neither was she.

That evening the house was gloomy in the dim candlelight and far too quiet. Tess missed having the TV turned on even though the guns on TV shows usually drove her right out of the room. She didn't mind worms or snakes or any of the usual girly-screamy things but she hated guns—they made her gut squirm. Guns, and gunfire. And the sound of guns on stupid cop shows. That evening, though, she would have been grateful for some stupid cop show for Daddy to watch, because of the silence. It wasn't like they were fighting, but—this was why she hardly ever went against Daddy, because he was all she had. Without him she was alone, a speck spinning in the universe. In the silence he seemed light-years away.

That night Tess had trouble getting to sleep. And when she finally dozed, the nightmare began. Something was wrong, something was wrong, nothing could ever be warm or safe or right again, the bedroom walls rippled and wavered like vertical water, and under them, or behind them, was—the wrong thing, the bad thing, that was going to take away—take away—take someone away—

She woke up.

Then she lay there with her heart urgently pounding because of the dream, because somehow the dream made her think of Kamo, Kam—where was he? She didn't know; that was what was wrong, more than anything. God, what an idiot she was, she had yelled at him, sent him away, and—maybe he was her brother, and even if he wasn't, she still felt—something, like he was maybe the one other person in the lonesome universe—but she had never found out where he lived, and she didn't know where or how to find him. What if he never came back?

6

She skipped school the next day and searched for him, starting around Hinkles Corner, asking at the post office and the video rental place and the Qwik Stop Gas & Lottery and the Paperback Trader. Most people she asked knew who Kam was and stared like they saw something branded on her forehead. Gossips. *They probably think he's fed me drugs or made me pregnant.* Just because he was a tough-looking stranger with long hair and scars.

People knew who Kamo was, but nobody seemed to know where to find him. And nobody had seen him that day.

Tess started asking at houses, up one long rickety set of steps to the front door and then down and then up the next one. Half the time nobody was home. The other half the time nobody could help her.

It got to be afternoon, and Tess hadn't eaten; her belly felt as achy and hollow as her chest. She gave up on Hinkles Corner and started hiking toward Canadawa, asking at houses along the way. On the far hills she could see school buses crawling like yellow caterpillars. She knocked at a farmhouse, asked about Kam. Walked on, asked at another. Another. Next minute, it seemed, she saw the sun hanging heavy like an egg yolk over the hills and realized she should have been at work.

Oh, God. She had to find Kam.

But—if she lost her job, forget everything. She and Daddy wouldn't eat.

Tess ran.

Had to get to work. She ran along the road, panting, her empty belly aching so badly she couldn't keep her legs going right. Eyes on the ground, she had to concentrate on every step, and she was miles away, and it was late, damn, she knew she was good and late. Hours late. Near the IGA finally, on the back alley that ran alongside the railroad right-of-way. Almost there, running like molasses up the delivery lot, past the Dumpster, toward the back door—

She heard gravelly scuffling noises, and looked up, and there were Butch and Kamo.

Kam.

Standing like a flint knife.

Butch in a white apron, hands to Kam's chest, shoving him around. Yelling stuff Tess couldn't understand at first; to her they were just sounds hanging on the air. "Get out! I'm tired of your ugly face hanging around."

There was no time to sort it out, what it was about,

why her heart was pounding. Tess kept running, toward them, and Butch was shoving Kam, making him stagger back, and Kam's hands were curled into fists, though he didn't lift them, and his face was hard, his single eye narrow and hard, though he kept his voice quiet. "I got a right—"

"Like I care? Sludge face." Butch grabbed Kam by the shoulders. "You get out of here. Now. Or I—"

"Stop it!" Tess didn't understand what was going on, but she knew she didn't like it. She barreled between them, knocking Butch's hands away from Kam. "Stop acting like jerks."

Butch stood back from Kamo, but he yelled at Tess like it was all her fault, "You don't call me a jerk!"

"I'm not. I—"

"Where you been! I told them you were sick."

"Tess," Kamo said, his voice quiet, surprised, warm, as if nothing were wrong now that she was there. "I been looking for you."

"Get the hell inside," Butch told her. He grabbed her by one arm and tried to propel her toward the stockroom door. She yanked her arm away.

"Stop it! I'm not going in. I've got to talk with Kam."

"What the hell for? You talk with freaks?" Butch tried to step past her to hassle Kam some more. She stood in his way. He glared, then turned and stomped into the IGA, slamming the door behind him.

Tess felt her knees go watery. Without meaning to,

she folded to sit on the gravel. Kam hunkered down and swiveled his lopsided face to peer at her.

"I'm sorry," he said.

"About what?" He hadn't done anything wrong that she knew of.

"Everything. How's your dad?"

His voice was too gentle. And she hadn't wanted to think about Daddy being sick, Daddy acting mad at her. Without warning tears started running down her face. She sobbed.

"Tess?" He sounded frightened. "Is it bad?"

"No," she managed to say through her sobbing. "He's okay."

Kamo put his arms around her.

It felt strange, yet right, having him close. She leaned against him. He patted her back and didn't say anything, just held her.

It felt good. But Tess hated to cry. What if somebody came out of the IGA and saw her? "Crap," she muttered, pulling away from Kam, rubbing her face, hiding behind her hands. Her face had to be as red as turkey wattles.

Kam crouched watching her.

"Daddy's okay," she told him. "He gets that way, and then he takes his pills, and then he's all right again." Until sometime maybe he wouldn't find his pills, or somebody would ask too many questions, maybe he wouldn't be all right. But Tess didn't want to think about it. "He's mad at me. Or upset. He's not talking." Daddy had hardly said a word to her that morning. "I been looking for you all day, and now my gut's killing me."

"You were looking for me?"

It had seemed like everything depended on finding him, yet Tess found she could not explain why. She fumbled for words without finding any, and God knew what he was thinking. She felt her face burn even redder.

He looked away from her, studying the hills, the locust trees standing black and feathery against the sky. He said, "You going to work?"

She shook her head. Couldn't go in there now, not with tear tracks on her smudgy red face.

"Home?"

"No. Daddy knows I'm supposed to be at work."

Kam seemed to understand that there were some things she couldn't explain to Daddy. He nodded. "C'mon," he said, and he stood up and stretched his right hand, the good one, down to her.

She got up without touching his hand. They walked silently up the steep road, out of Hinkles Corner, down through the salvage yard and past the sawmill. Tess began to suspect he was taking her home after all. "Where we going?"

"Dinner."

They cut through the woods, came out in an abandoned pasture, and headed downhill between clumps of sassafras and honeysuckle toward the creek. Tess could see an oxbow of water shining in the low light. But halfway down to the river bottom, Kam rounded an outcropping of rock and turned toward a run-in shed cows had once used. When they reached it he ducked inside, and Tess realized it was his camp.

He had a tarp on the ground, and some blankets to sleep in, and a blanket spread over a muddle of stuff in a back corner, and cardboard tacked up over the drafty places in the walls. A roof to keep off rain, three walls—it could have been worse. The open side was screened by sumac, so he had some privacy. Tess noticed a black circle of ground inside a ring of stones where he'd built a campfire. No fear that anybody would see. There was nothing around but pasture and woods, no houses or anything, for probably a mile.

Kam got on his knees near the fire ring, rummaging in a knapsack. Tess stood and watched as he pulled out a packet of graham crackers, and her stomach started to howl like a chained dog.

"C'mon in, sit down," he said. He handed her the crackers and kept rummaging. "I'll get the fire going and cook us some soup." He pulled out a couple of dented cans of store-brand beef-and-barley condensed.

Tess settled in with her back against an upright and gulped graham crackers. Kam had firewood ready, stacked along the back of the run-in shed to stay dry. She sat, eating more slowly once her belly quieted down, and watched him break a punky dead branch into kindling.

He said, "That guy at the IGA must like you." He

looked up from his kindling and gave her a flicker of a smile. "He acts jealous as a rooster."

If Kam was trying to make her feel better, he was succeeding. Butch, an actual boy, seemed to like her? But—nah. Tess said, "That's just the way Butch is. Acts like he owns the place."

"He's territorial, all right." Kam crumpled a piece of newspaper, tented slivers of punk wood over it, and lit a match to it. The paper blazed, then dwindled. Little flames licked up from the wood. Kam fed finger-thick sticks to the small fire, then pulled a dented metal pot out of his knapsack, got up, and headed down through hoppleberry bushes to the creek. In a few minutes he came back with the pot full of water and said, "Thank you for getting him out of my face. You keep saving my ass. Thank you."

He seemed to mean it. Tess set down the graham crackers in surprise. "You could have handled him."

"Maybe." He crouched to open the soup cans. "I'd rather not. I'll stay out of a fight whenever I can."

"You—you will?"

"Not much punch in this." He lifted his withered hand and glanced at her. "Guys like whatsisname, Butch, they scare me." His shoulders shivered. "Anything happens to the good eye, that's it, I'm blind."

She shuddered with him. Okay, it made sense. Of course he wasn't a fighter.

But—she had thought—

Tess blurted out, "What happened to your other eye?"

Mixing soup, his hands stopped moving. He canted his head and looked up at her. The sun was going down, putting Kam and everything inside the cowshed into shadow. Firelight flickered on his face; shadows moved but he didn't. Tess couldn't tell what he was thinking or feeling. He stared so long she thought he wasn't going to answer, like she shouldn't have asked the question.

He said, "My stepfather."

At first she didn't understand. Then she started to understand, and she couldn't speak.

Oh, my God. It happened when—when he was just a little kid.

"He killed the eye just hitting me all the time," Kam said.

She didn't want to believe she had heard him right. "Your—your stepfather? Your own family?"

"Beat me silly whenever he felt like it." Hard and blunt as creek stones.

"God," Tess whispered. "Kam, that's awful."

He tilted his head down. He turned back to fixing soup.

She said, "Your scars—" She hated to ask, but she needed to know. He was Kam, he was just right, he was the greatest thing since somebody took electricity and ran it through a guitar, yet—nothing about him was making sense to her. He was tough, yet—he wasn't a tough guy at all? "Your hand—"

"He did that too."

She didn't ask how. "Was it—like—the whole time you were a kid—"

"As long as I can remember he beat me. I left when I was twelve."

God.

"Been on my own pretty much ever since."

Her chest hurt for him, her mind hurt. *It shouldn't have happened.* "Where was your mother? Dead?" *Like mine?*

Kam placed his cooking pot carefully on the dirt floor. He got up and brought two small logs from his stack of firewood. He added a few sticks to his campfire, keeping it small; it was already burning down. He placed the logs one on each side of it and balanced the pot on them, over the embers. He did not look at Tess.

He said, very low, "She was right there all the time. She let him hurt me."

Something sizzled. With a shock Tess saw that Kamo was silently crying. His face did not move, but his scarred cheek shone in the firelight, wet. His tears were falling on the hot ashes at the edge of the fire.

"I'm sorry," she whispered. She didn't know what else to say. Her hand lifted toward him, but stopped; maybe he would not want to be touched.

"She would feed me cookies afterward," Kam said, his voice stretched tight and hard, like a drumhead.

"I'm sorry." Maybe he knew what she meant.

He nodded. "She's probably still with him." He left his

soup on the fire and sat back, facing Tess. He made no effort to wipe away the tears or hide them. "Hell," he said.

She nodded. "So you got out."

"Not soon enough."

She waited. He went on.

"What happened was, when I got to be bigger, eleven, twelve, I started to fight back. Made it worse. He beat me so bad sometimes I thought I was gonna die—but one night, the son of a bitch was so drunk when he came after me that I got him down. I got him down on the floor. And then I had to decide." Kam faltered. His gaze slipped away from her. Looking at the fire, slowly he said, "I wanted to kill him. I wanted to do him the way he did me and then kill him slow."

Tess felt her breath congeal in her chest. Twelve years old, he had been forced to decide whether to be a murderer.

Kam glanced up at her. "See, the ironic thing is, usually kids who get beat up, like me—they grow up to be just like the people who did it to them."

But not Kamo. With uncanny sureness Tess knew what he had decided, and she knew his mind was strong enough to make it stick. "You didn't kill him," she said. "You didn't want to be like him. You ran away to look for your father."

He ducked his head. He lifted his arm and scrubbed away the tears with his sleeve.

Tess decided it was time for her to shut up. She sat

back, leaned her head against the shed wall and closed her eyes. The soup was starting to heat up; it smelled good. So did the smoke. So did the faint, sweet, grassy aroma of cows that still came up from the ground. Tess heard a quiet slow-dance rhythm start inside her head, yet at the same time she was thinking. About Kam. About what his life had been like.

He had been serious when he told her nobody had ever loved him.

He needed to find his father.

She opened her eyes. He was stirring the soup. "Kam," she asked, "you sticking around?"

He looked over at her and nodded. "A little while longer. There's something I have to do."

Tess knew she had to help him. And she had an idea how. It scared her—but she knew what she had to do.

Daddy was in bed, asleep, when she got home. Since he didn't have TV to watch, he got bored in the evenings and went to bed early. Or maybe he was still in his silent mood and didn't want to talk to her. Fine. She wouldn't have to deal with him until morning.

Tess felt bone tired, her head ached from too much to think about, and all she wanted in the world was a hot shower. Instead, she bathed at the pump, shivering and muttering to herself. Forget hot showers for the foreseeable future, especially if she had lost her job. Damn, she hated being poor, she hated it, she hated it! All her life, or at least all her life that she remembered, it had been poor, poor, poor, government-surplus cheese and powdered milk, which tastes putrid, and brush the teeth with baking soda, which tastes even worse, and don't lose the pencil the teacher gives you. . . . Store-bought clothes? Forget that. Get by with secondhand. Being poor was supposed to give a person character, and Tess knew this was true because she sure was the school character in all those funky old clothes. Which was another reason why, damn it, she wanted things. She wanted a CD player and the Crux CD, she wanted a Walkman, she wanted some real clothes—all right, mostly she wanted jeans, brand-name jeans so the other kids would stop thinking she was contagiously and terminally uncool.

She wanted—a chance.

She went to bed and lay there twitching her fingers in time with the rhythms going in her head, trying not to think. She went to sleep.

The nightmare came, as she knew it would. Just a little different this time. The walls were soot black and solid brick. Gloomy, but strong. They would never give way.

Yet they moved, they bulged, the dull black paint cracked, the brick started to crack, and Tess was scared—

Don't wake up.

Even in her sleep, Tess knew what she had to do to help Kamo. She was going to take charge of her dream. Whenever she had her nightmare she was going to stick with it and—find out. Find out what it was about. Whatever was walled in, hidden away from her and trying to get out—that was the scary stuff she couldn't remember, and it was time to remember. She wanted to remember. For Kam.

The black brick walls thinned and rippled and turned to a black curtain. And behind it there was something—terrifying—

Don't wake up!

She stuck with it. The next moment, it was as if the curtain pulled away, like she was watching a play, and she could see—the rectangle of sunlight as a door opened, and she could almost see—the man—silhouetted in the—doorway—

Then there was a red explosion, a black scream, someone crying. Tess woke up, gasping and sweating, her heart pounding, feeling dizzy weak shaky like in school once when some girl with asthma had given her a whiff of her inhaler, except this was worse—she felt like a heart attack case, a candidate for one of Daddy's pills. She sat up in bed, trying to calm down, afraid to go back to sleep if she had to face the red-and-black terror again.

Just a nightmare.

No, dammit, not a nightmare, really. A memory. Walled in. She knew that now.

It's too hard. I can't do this.

Yet—she had to try. She had to keep trying. For Kam. For herself.

— 64 —

7

"So where were you so late?"

It was breakfast time, there was bread but no margarine, and Tess couldn't quite tell whether Daddy was in a better mood or not. He was trying to be. He was talking to her. He was keeping his voice down, keeping it light. But there was worry in his eyes.

Tess didn't exactly answer. "Daddy, I wasn't that late. You went to bed early."

"I never heard you come in."

"You went to sleep." She tried to tease. "It's hard to hear anything when you're asleep. Hard to tell what time it is when the clocks don't work, either."

He nodded, smiled, changed the subject, letting it go. They talked about the Phillies, losing again, as usual. They talked about making some pork and sauerkraut sometime if pork shanks went on sale. He kept looking at her as they talked.

She asked him to sign a blank piece of notebook paper for her because she needed a note for a field trip. He knew she was lying, she could tell he knew. But he didn't say anything. He signed it. She wrote herself an excuse and used it to get back into school that day.

After school, and after getting called to the guidance office as usual when the deficiency notices went out, she hiked to the IGA to see whether she still had a job, and she did. Butch had said she was sick. They knew she didn't have a phone. It was okay. So Tess went back to the stockroom to get to work.

Butch was there. "Hey," he said, flashing his famous grin at her. "You notice I didn't tell them anything."

She had expected him to be mad at her, like yesterday. But he wasn't. And she still had her job. She smiled at him.

"I'll buy you a soda over break," he said.

She wanted to read magazines over break. There was a special issue of *Rolling Stone* all about Crux—nobody knew who this guy was and they could still write about him, like what the songs were supposed to mean, and what the name "Crux" was supposed to mean, what kind of cross, like the Christ cross or a pagan universe symbol or a tree of life or an ankh or the constellation Southern Cross or what? Or just an X, like a poor man's mark? Tess had read the article and she wanted to read it again, she wanted to memorize it. But Crux was just a dream, right? Here was a real boy saying he was going to buy her a soda. A cute boy. A popular boy.

"Sure," she answered, even though what he'd said hadn't sounded like a question. "Thanks."

She worked till closing that night. Then slept like a sack of potatoes, no nightmares. Was back at the IGA at eight the next morning, Saturday, and worked all day.

She looked for Kam at breaks but didn't worry when he wasn't there. He had said he was sticking around. Anyway, she had nothing to tell him yet.

Every two hours "Secret Star" came on the radio and Tess stopped whatever she was doing to listen. The song made her breathless every time. Strong words, but it was the strong, complicated rhythms that made her tingle—those, and the strong, wild voice. She'd know that voice anywhere. She played it in her head. She heard it sometimes in her dreams.

"I've got the CD," Butch told her.

The last couple of days Butch was being so nice Tess was beginning to think maybe he really did like her. It seemed impossible, but if that wasn't it, what was going on? He had bought her a Pepsi, a Milky Way bar, an ice cream sandwich. He talked with her while they were working and during breaks. He told her things. Like her, Butch didn't have a mother. His father traveled a lot making speeches. His father expected him to go into one of the military academies after high school.

At the back of her mind, Tess had always kind of believed in the Cinderella story, all those romantic stories where the boy was bad like a wild stallion but he was good to the girl so the girl knew he really loved her, love like a miracle that changed her life. Tess's life needed help so bad, maybe Butch was her miracle. Maybe Butch was going to make her his girlfriend, make her popular. Maybe Butch was her prince.

"The Crux CD," Butch said. "I have it."

"You twit. I hate you."

He took this the way she intended it, as friendly envy. "You want to hear it?"

"Nooooo." As if he didn't know she about wet her pants every time Crux came on the radio. Butch knew she wanted to hear that Crux album worse than anything.

"I'll play it for you after work."

She was supposed to go home. Daddy would have supper waiting. But she would have walked through razor wire to hear that CD. Tess said, "Okay."

"I'll show you my room. I got all sorts of things you'll like." Butch sauntered off.

Lupe was listening. When Butch was far enough away she said softly, "Tess. You know, he is the kind—I hear him talking to his friends. It is all about what he does to girls. How he scores."

But that was just the way the popular boys tried to impress each other. "He likes to talk big," Tess said. "He's not a bad guy, really. Don't worry. I'll be fine."

Butch drove one of those pickups on huge wheels, Tess noted, the kind with lollipop lights and a roll bar. Instead of taking her straight to hear the CD he took her to Canadawa first and bought her a burger and fries to go at the Hot'N'Now. Then he headed out via twisty hill-country back roads, driving so fast it was hard to eat. But finally he and Tess got to his house.

Tess hadn't realized till then that Butch was rich, at least by her standards. In a fancy development, the house was big as a barn and shiny as a Cadillac. Butch's father wasn't home. Sure, Tess realized, most fathers weren't home much, not like Daddy was always home for her, but what was it like walking every day into that big barn of an empty house? Who was he supposed to talk to, the cleaning service? Butch's kid sister was home, but when she saw him coming in with a girl she went to her room and stayed there.

Butch took Tess by the hand. "In here," he said, tugging her down a long hallway toward his bedroom.

When they got into his room he led her to the bed. Tess felt funny sitting on Butch's bed, but there was nowhere else to sit. No desk or chair, though a whole wall of the room was taken up by a monster piece of furniture holding TV and VCR and a sound system with three-foot speakers and piles of videos and CDs. No wonder he had the Crux CD—he probably bought every CD that came out. Butch didn't need a job at the IGA. Big house, big stereo, DAT deck, he had plenty of money. Tess wondered why he bothered to work at all. Maybe just so he had people to talk to and something to do.

He closed the door and put on the Crux CD and

turned it up loud enough so she could hear it with her whole body.

Right from the first note Tess was gone. It didn't matter that she was sitting on Butch's bed, or that he sat down next to her and slid closer to her and started talking to her; she nodded and smiled and didn't hear a word he said. All she heard was Crux, the messages in his words and his salt-and-sugar voice and the red-and-blue rhythms of his guitar—nobody else played guitar like he did, and the music mags she read during breaks at the IGA were full of stupid articles by experts trying to figure out how he did it. His chords, his finger-picking—the whole sound of his music was different and shivery and awesome; she could have listened to him all night and day. She was drumming along with Crux, tapping out rhythms on her knees, kicking the floor, pounding on the edge of the mattress as the tempo rose. Most of the time she didn't even notice that Butch was there.

Tess wanted—something she didn't have the words to name, but she felt it when she looked at the cover of the Crux CD, a lonesome four-rayed star floating in a midnight sky that was the huge pupil of an indigo eye. She wanted—she wanted to fly or something. She wanted more than just stupid dreams, but that was all she had, dreams. One magazine at the store had had a contest for artists to come up with pictures of what they thought the secret star looked like, and some of the pictures were as if the artists knew her dreams of him. One woman painted him crucified on a guitar. Another woman showed him as a constellation dancing along with all the old Greek stuff that was supposed to be up in the sky, gods and swans and sheep and lions and bulls. Some man painted him riding a palomino horse bareback through a sunset city, blond hair blending with the horse's wild mane and the evening star rising in the tawny sky. Each artist made him look diferent, yet he was always perfect, always angel-beautiful, always guitar-god mountaintop take-my-breath-away—transcendent, that was the word—like his songs.

Tess wanted—hope? A life? Him? Listening to his music made her heart ache, yet whatever it was she needed, he was there, giving it to her.

When the CD stopped, though, Crux wasn't there anymore. Butch was.

All too real and solid, there he was, pressed against her with his arm around her shoulders.

"Okay, baby, my turn," he said, and he mashed his face into hers.

"Hey!" She shoved him away. "What the—"

"C'mon, baby, you know you're crazy about me." He tackled her with both arms, toppling her back onto the bed, and there he was on top of her, his hips heavy on hers, jamming his mouth into her face.

He was big and brawny, made of solid muscle. "Stop it!" Tess screamed at him, squirming to get free, but with his weight on top of her she could barely move. He had her arms pinned, she couldn't get her hands on him, but she could bite, and she did. Hard.

"Hey!" He flinched away.

"Get—off—me!" Once she finally got some leverage she threw him halfway across the room. He landed on his butt on the rug, and she stood over him so scorching mad she couldn't say half of what she was thinking. The—the consummate jerkhead, where did he get off thinking he could grab her like that? "You've got no right," she panted at him.

"Bitch! You hurt me!" There was blood on his face.

"Oh, poor *baby!*" She slammed out.

She got halfway down his driveway before he came after her in the truck. "Crazy bitch, what's the matter with you?" he yelled.

"Nothing's the matter with *me.*"

"Slut! Get in here!"

Oh, that made a lot of sense. She wouldn't give him what he wanted, so now she was a slut? And she was supposed to get back in his truck so he could take her somewhere and try again? Right. Sure. "Go kiss yourself," she told him, striding along as fast as she could without running from him.

Butch called her several more names before he revved the truck and roared away. "You can bloody walk home!" he screamed at her.

She did.

It was late when she got back, but her cold dinner was still on the table and Daddy was still up, sitting in the dark living room with nothing but a burned-down candle and Ernestine for company. With his lips pressed together. "You're grounded," he said.

Tess looked at him with no heart to try to explain. There was no such thing as a prince, she was angry at herself for ever having thought there was, and her mouth felt filthy from Butch no matter how much she scrubbed at it with her hand, her whole face felt filthy from Butch. She felt filthy all over.

Daddy was watching her for a reaction, and he seemed to see guilt in her face; his bald spot went dark and he swelled up in his chair. "You've been messing around with that bum Kamo!" he yelled. "I knew it, and I won't have it! He's not welcome here, and he's not welcome near you."

All of a sudden Tess was nearly as furious at Daddy as she had been at Butch. She wanted to hit something, it was so frustrating, this whole nuisance of being a girl. Butch thinking he could score with her. Daddy thinking that was what she'd been doing. "For God's sake!" she screamed. "What do you think I am?"

"I don't—"

"Kamo might be my brother! You think I'd—"

"He's not your brother!"

"Like you know that!"

"I do know that. He's not your brother. He's not any relation to you."

This was too important to shout about. "How do you know?" Tess asked, almost whispering.

Daddy's voice came down as well. "I just know. He's not related to you."

"Daddy—"

"He's not, Tess. That's all I'm going to say." Daddy swung around and zoomed Ernestine into his bedroom. He closed the door.

Tess blew out the candle and stood in the dark thinking, trying to figure out how much to believe. She wanted to believe whatever Daddy said—but how could she anymore? There was too much he wasn't telling her.

That night after she finally got to sleep she had the nightmare again and tried to see it through. But it got all mixed up with Butch somehow and she woke up knowing nothing except that she wanted Kam, she needed to see Kam, he was the only one she could really talk with, she had to see him, and how could she? She was grounded.

In the morning things went both better and worse than Tess expected. Better because Daddy had French toast ready when she got up, with syrup made from brown sugar. Tess knew what this meant: she was forgiven. "I was crabby last night when you came in," he said as she sat down to eat, which meant she wasn't grounded after all and was about as close as he ever got to apologizing.

"It's all right," Tess said, and for a moment it was.

"Had a bad day yesterday," Daddy explained. "And it seems like you're never around anymore to help me out."

She looked at him with her mouth full of French toast and grew aware that French toast was nothing but soggy flabby bread sweetened with sugar water. "What kind of bad day?"

"My chest hurt. I had to push on over to Millers' for help, and for a couple minutes I felt like me and Ernestine weren't going to make it."

Tess stopped chewing and sat there staring at him.

"Just angina, the doc says. But now we got doc bills, and a whiz-bang emergency room bill, and a new kind of pill bill, and you wouldn't believe how much them suckers cost. And the Medicare don't cover all of it."

Chewing again, she didn't taste the food, and her stomach felt like something heavy had just landed in it: all the things Daddy hadn't said.

Like, there was never going to be enough money for anything, no matter how much she worked at the IGA.

Like, the more she grew up and got herself a life, the more he was going to be alone.

Like, he was afraid of dying. He was feeling old and afraid.

He said, "I'm starting to think we're going to have to unload this place after all, Tess. Get an apartment in town someplace where there'll be people around and I can get to the doctors' offices and the welfare offices and maybe I can find some kind of job."

Welfare? Apartment? Move in town? But—this was home. There were trees out back, hills, room to breathe. Deer, wildcats, hawks, red foxes in the rocks. Anyhow, they had just cleaned the cistern. Her voice came out a whisper when she said to Daddy, "You're giving up. Don't give up."

Move in town? You could barely even see the stars at night in town.

"Got to, Tess. I'm getting up there, I gotta be realistic. But you're young, you shouldn't be worrying about an old poop like me, you should be going to school—"

"Oh, *right*." She got up and headed outside and walked into the woods so she wouldn't have to hear any more of this.

It had rained overnight. Little white starflowers, so dainty they were practically see-through, were coming up from the black mossy ground like a promise. They didn't help. She tried playing "Secret Star" in her mind.

> *In this dirty world*
> *you can't see far*
> *but you gotta believe*
> *there's a secret star*

But she couldn't believe anymore. There was no secret star for people like Daddy and her. They were dug into a hole so deep she couldn't see a twinkle of light. There was no way out. They would never get the electricity back, or the phone. No amount of working at a minimum-wage job would ever pay the bills. Next the house would go. They were just sliding down, down, like in a coal chute. Might as well give it up and live in a cowshed like Kam.

8

It was her day off, Sunday, and she wasn't grounded after all, yet Tess didn't feel as if she could go see Kamo. She went back inside and sat staring at the clutter spread everywhere because Daddy couldn't reach things if they were put away, and the scars on the paneling and doors from his wheelchair, and the blank screen of the TV, and Mom's picture on top of it staring back at her. Daddy kept her studio portrait there. Sometimes when he forgot Tess was around she would hear him talking to the picture. "Miss ya, babe," he would say. "Ain't nobody never been so beautiful." Her name was Teresa Riordan Rojahin Mathis, and she was spectacular. Green eyes, honey-colored hair, sweet face with a tiny Mona Lisa smile. "But I'm doing okay," Daddy would tell her. "Hanging in there."

Dumb, Tess scolded herself. She had been stupid to think Butch could actually like her. Stupid to think even in her wildest dreams that anybody was ever going to love her the way Daddy still loved her mother. *Why did I have to turn out like a palomino ox instead of like her?* Looking at Mom didn't make Tess feel any better. She didn't remember her. Looking at her was like looking at a photo in a magazine.

Lunchtime came and passed, but there was nothing to eat except leftover French toast, so nobody ate. Daddy sat at the kitchen table playing solitaire with a deck that had a joker instead of an ace of hearts. Tess sat where she was.

Outside, the day was the color of dirty hubcaps. Getting set to rain.

In the gray light an orange blob pulled into the weedy gravel driveway.

"Who the—" Tess looked. It was an old VW bus, what kids call a hippie bus. There was a black guy with dreadlocks driving. Somebody got out of the passenger side: Kam.

"Oh, my God." Her first thought was that he'd give Daddy a heart attack just by being there. She bolted up and ran out to tell him to go away before Daddy saw him. But something about his face stopped her. He was smiling. Downright grinning, his wide mouth and one eye as happy as a long day of sunshine. She had never seen him like that before.

"Hey, Tess!" He hugged her, then let go again before she could blink. "Meet Joshua." The black guy was opening the back doors of the van. He smiled and waved at her. Kam said, "Give us a hand?"

— 79 —

"With what?"

"You'll see." Kam led her around back of the van and lifted out—a drum.

It was a metallic-blue Pearl-brand bass drum. Kam handed it to Tess and said, "Happy birthday," even though it wasn't her birthday. Then he reached into the van again and pulled out—a tom-tom.

And Joshua was standing there with lengths of chrome-plated drum stand in his hands, saying to Kam, "Where should we set it up, man?"

Kam looked at Tess, but her mouth was stuck in a half-open position and wasn't functioning. He looked at the house, where Daddy had wheeled his chair into the doorway, maybe just to watch but maybe to block it—and then Kamo smiled even wider and said, "How about right here in the yard?"

"You say so." The two of them moved to the center of the crabgrassy patch in front of the house and started setting up—it was a drum set, a whole hot-rockin' four-drum set with crash cymbal and ride cymbal, the works. Tess had never gotten to play on a real complete drum set in her life, not even in school.

"Yo! Tess, bring that bass," Kam sang. Tess walked but felt as if she were floating, as if the sound of his voice carried her to him. She loved his voice. Usually it was made of shadows, but that moment it was made of rainbows and silver.

He looked the drum over before he set it in its place.

All the dampers were there on the insides of the skins. "Not bad for secondhand," he remarked.

Not bad? That sparkly-blue, heaven-colored drum?

"Grab the hi-hat out of the van," Joshua suggested, smiling the way Kamo was.

"Can you bring the stool, Tess?" Kam called.

There was so much wonderfulness she couldn't carry it all at once. Floor tom-tom, snare drum, foot pedals, sticks, extra sticks with plastic tips. Kam came to help.

"Hey!" He looked at her face and hugged her again, longer this time. "No big deal, Tess. Just helping the dude clean out his garage. C'mon, try it out."

Her heart was aching fit to split right in her chest, because she was feeling two things at once: Lord-God happy, because Kamo was giving her this wonderful thing—and deep-purple sad, because she knew she and Daddy needed other things more, and maybe she ought to sell the drums, maybe doing that would bring enough money for—some of the bills or something . . .

"Tickle it, Tess!" Kam urged.

She was going to play it at least this once, right there on the front lawn. She settled her bottom on the stool, hugged the snare drum between her legs, positioned her feet on the pedals, balanced the sticks in her hands and closed her eyes a minute to think how she was going to do this, because it had been awhile since she had played on anything except scrub buckets. But the rhythms were jumping like lottery balls in her head, and she started the big, thick ride cymbal going right along with them, eight quick beats to the frame.

Then she got the bass going, twos and fours. Then she started to fill in left-handed with everything else that was bubbling in her brain, and her left foot was pumping the hi-hat in time with the snare, and as usual she couldn't quite quick-lick it all in but she was cooking, she was smoking hot, she kept getting closer and closer, which was just about as good as it gets, and she didn't care how the hi-hat's telescoping stand kept sinking down or how she looked with her big butt bouncing around on that stool—the little drum angels were dancing like popcorn behind her eyes, and just because she felt like it she smacked the crash cymbal and boiled into a riff, chopping on the side of the snare and whacking an open-mouth ping out of the hi-hat and skittering the sticks all around the set like witches whirling under a full moon.

Standing there, Kam arched his back and threw back his head so his hair trailed down. "Whoo-eee *mama!*" he yelled to the sky.

"*Rock* steady," Joshua said, crouching on his haunches and listening. He had been smirking when Tess started, but she could see he wasn't anymore, and now Tess knew she was real.

She knew she couldn't sell the drum set, damn it. Not for any money. Some things were more important than—than . . .

She stopped drumming. Swiveled around on her stool

to look at Daddy. He hadn't spoken, he hadn't ordered Kamo or the drum set off his land—yet.

Benson Mathis had been thinking. Since the night Kamo had said "Rojahin" to him he had been thinking a lot.

There was what he wanted, which was for Kam to go away and things to be like they were before. But then there was what he knew to be true, which was that things would never be the same. There was what he feared, which was that Tess would hate him when she found out. But then again there was what he knew to be true, which was that he had to let Tess grow and he had to let her go.

In strong moments he was getting to the heart of the matter, which was not so much what to do or what might happen as what it meant for him to be a man.

Nothing had prepared him for this. Back when he had legs he could stand on, being a man had meant carrying the most weight, earning a bigger paycheck, holding his own in a fight. It had meant getting through boot camp okay, serving his country and coming home again and not talking about it too much. It had meant winning his woman. It had meant defending and protecting her. Right up to the minute they had put him in this wheelchair he had known what it meant to be a man.

But now—what the hell was he? Kamo had looked to him like he was still a man, and he had let the kid down.

Kamo was looking to him again. So was Tess. Finished playing her new drum set, turning to see what he thought, and Lord God Almighty was she good. What was it going to mean for her to be a woman?

Benson Mathis knew he had to do better for her than he'd been managing lately. He flexed his shoulders and got himself moving, got Ernestine rolling out of the doorway, across the flat doorstep and onto the grass. Finding the heart of the problem, he had found his own heart, and he felt it warming him. He felt himself smiling.

He looked Kam in the eye. He felt his voice come out dry and friendly as he said, "What kind of damn fool would set up drums in the yard?" He said, "Kids today, got no sense. Crazy. For God's sake bring those drums inside before it starts to rain."

That night it happened again. Tess's dream. The walls, the strong walls that were supposed to hold out the bad thing, thinned and started wavering, going black, blowing like shadows in the wind.

Don't wake up.

She could almost see, now, what lay behind. She could see—a man, a golden man, coming in the door with his hand raised, his face—she wanted to see his face—

Stay with it.

But then—then all she could see was the other man in the dark corner—and—she was just a kid, sitting on the stairs and looking down between the rails, frightened—but why? The man in the corner was just Daddy talking with Kam, the two of them as cautious as strange dogs getting acquainted, the way they had been all evening, Kam saying *There's something I have to do,* Kam saying *Gotta go now,* but Daddy—Daddy was not in his wheelchair, why not? Standing there, reaching for his pocket, saying *Get out!* and she—she wanted to shake and cry and hide so she wouldn't have to see, yet even as she watched from inside the nightmare she knew the future, knew she was going to be left all alone, she knew—she knew she would never see the most important person in her world again—

She woke up as if a gun had gone off by her ear, feeling achy and abandoned. Then she knew. She sat straight up in bed, gasping, knowing clear to her bones what she had been too excited all evening to recognize.

Something I have to do, Kam had said the other day. Just because she had tried to be a friend, he felt like he had to do something for her. Before he went away.

The drums were Kamo's way of saying good-bye.

9

Heart thudding, she bolted out of bed and into her shirt, her jeans, her boots. She ran out the door, not even caring whether Daddy heard her thundering out in the middle of the night, whether he would worry. Let him worry. She had to find Kam before it was too late.

Joshua had gone off in his van soon after he had brought the drums, but Kam had stayed till dusk. He was on foot. He would have gone back to his camp to get his things. Maybe—maybe there was still time.

Of course it had to be a cloudy night, no light at all. No moon, no stars, just darkness with entirely too many hard objects in it. Trees. Roots and rocks to trip over. Obstacles, like ditches and drops and streams. Tess tried to go through the woods, but in the dark it was like combat. She had to retreat. Found the road and loped along on blind faith, figuring as long as her feet slapped down on asphalt she was okay, sobbing the whole time, barely able to breathe as she kept running. Every once in a while there was a farm with its security lights on so she knew where she was. But it was eerie quiet. Not one car passed. The only sounds she heard were herself, crying, and farm dogs barking as her thumping feet ran by.

When she got near Hinkles Corner she ran like a runaway truck down through the salvage yard and the sawmill yard, where there were lights, and then she charged on into the woods. No light there, not a glimmer, but this neck of woods was not too wide. She fought her way through and went rushing down the overgrown pasture, tramping through cedars and honeysuckle toward Kamo's camp.

He was still there. Thank God, he was still there. On the dark air she could hear his radio, sweet and clear, playing a Crux song.

Then it stopped. He had heard something coming, crashing along like a moose.

Tess slowed down a little and got herself under enough control so she wasn't bawling like a moose too. It was okay. It was okay. She could see Kamo's campfire now, burned down to embers, guiding her to his camp like an oversized golden star somehow knocked to the black ground.

She blundered her way up to it, and there he was, sitting very still on the other side of the glowing coals, and the way the faint light found him she felt for a minute as if his face were floating in the black night, a tawny butterfly lifting toward her.

"Kam." She could barely talk, she was panting so

hard. "Kam, don't go." He was packed to leave, she could tell even in the dark. The rope he had hung his clothes on was gone from under the eaves. No pots sat by the fire. His knapsack bulged.

He stood up, and his face blinked out. All she could see were his jeans from the knee down and his booted feet.

"Kam, please. Don't go away." Still crying, damn it. "I'm working on it, I—I'm so close. I can almost remember."

He kicked dirt over the fire. She couldn't see, didn't know where he was.

"Kamo!"

"I'm right here." His gruff voice sounded near her ear. He stood beside her and put an arm around her shoulders—just one arm, light and easy, but it was as if he were made of peace. Calmness seeped through her from his touch. Gently he turned her, aiming her toward home, and he started her walking. He walked beside her with his arm lightly riding on her.

"Your daddy's never gonna forgive me now," he teased. "Leading you astray. You're out running around in the night, and he's gonna fetch his shotgun. He and Ernestine are gonna hunt me down."

"Don't go," Tess said.

He sighed. She could feel the sigh run like a soft drumroll through his warm shoulder. He said, "I have to keep looking for him."

His daddy, he meant. She said, "I'm telling you, I'm almost there. I'm going to remember."

"You been—trying to force yourself?"

"Kind of."

He stopped walking, faced her even though they could barely see each other in the darkness and put both hands on her shoulders. "How come?"

"I have to do something, don't I?"

"No, you don't. Not for me. Listen, if you're gonna remember, you got to do it for yourself."

She had thought he would be grateful. She flared at him, "I'll do it for you if I want to!"

"It might—it might hurt you, Tess."

"I don't care!"

He turned and started walking again. Taking her home the back way, toward the creek bottom, he didn't blunder into a thing. He walked through the dark like a cat. Sometimes he seemed barely human. Where did this guy come from? Who was he? Trying to figure him out was as frustrating as trying to see into her dreams. Tess demanded, "What the heck kind of name is Kamo, anyway?"

With a quirk in his voice he shot back, "What kind of name is Tessali?"

"So my mother got in a poetic mood." Girls were allowed to have weird names. "I'm serious, Kam. What flavor are you? Greek or something?"

He sighed again. "I don't really know."

It sounded like his mother hadn't told him much more about this Rojahin man than Daddy had told her. Tess tried another question. "What kind of musician? You said your father was a musician."

"Played piano in a bar." He said it without a hint of put-down, and she had a kind of flash, almost a vision, of a little boy sitting right under the piano, awash in the music, feeling it, breathing it, and how melodies must have come down like thundershowers, and how big and wonderful that piano-playing daddy must have seemed.

"Then—your mother left him, or he left her—"

"Right. One of those things."

"And—you never saw him again."

"Since I was five. Right."

There were questions she didn't want to ask, but he heard them in her silence.

"The way my stepfather was, Tess—it was no damn wonder my father never came to see me."

But the father should have been there. He shouldn't have left his son to a stepfather who beat him. It was illogical that Kam could forgive his father for doing nothing when he blamed his mother for the same thing.

Kam said, "I'm scared I'm gonna find out he's dead. Nothing left but a white wooden cross along some roadside, where he drove himself into some ditch, the way he used to drink. But then—I'm scared I'm gonna find him still around, and he just didn't care." His voice was going thin. "Dead would be better."

So he did think about it.

They didn't say much the rest of the way back. She could have told him about Butch, but she never thought of it; Butch wasn't important. She'd handled him. Far up a hillside she heard a deep-voiced owl crooning, and far down the creek bottom a fox yipped, singing high and thin as a new moon.

By the time they reached the Mathis place the cloudy sky was starting to lighten from black to rainy gray. At the edge of the backyard Kam faced her.

"Kamo," she whispered, "please stay."

In the quicksilver dawn light she could see him looking back at her. For some reason he seemed afraid, as if she could do something to him. Didn't he know she would never hurt him?

"Just a few more days," she begged.

She saw his jaw tighten. But he nodded.

"Don't go without telling me."

He nodded again. It was a promise.

It rained all that day. Tess got soaking wet hiking to the IGA after school.

She walked in, and Butch looked straight at her and said, "Bitch."

She didn't care. She was so falling-down tired from being up half the night that she could barely keep moving. She was too tired to do anything about Butch, even if she knew what to do.

"I'll get you, bitch," he said to her, low and mean, when nobody was listening. "No slut disses me. I'll get your snotty ass."

All through shift he was like that. During break she couldn't go outside to get away from him, because it was raining. Yawning, she went up front to look at the *Rolling Stone* special issue on Crux.

She was dreaming about Crux wild-haired on a far-away mountaintop, under a shadowy moon, singing rhythm and blues with the wolves, when somebody grabbed her nasty-hard by the arm. "Bitch," somebody hissed in her ear.

Tess knew who it was. She yanked her arm out of his grip, whirled around, and caught him by the front of his shirt. All of a sudden she had her energy back and she was blazing mad. She got a fistful of shirt and hauled him close to her face so she could make an impression on him without yelling. "Butch," she told him very softly and sweetly, "you are being a colossal jerk. Let me alone."

He tore away, ripping his shirt. His face had gone clay white. "You are gonna die," he said, his voice choked as if she had strangled him. His hand shot to his pants pocket.

Tess heard jeering. Looking in the plate-glass window were half a dozen guys, high-school kids she recognized, Butch's friends. Butch had been trying to show off in front of them, apparently, and they were yowling and meowing and laughing ha-ha.

For just a moment Butch looked so much like a cornered little boy that she actually felt sorry for him. "Look," she told him, "you let me alone and I let you alone. It's that simple."

He didn't seem to think so. His hand gripped his pocket. "You're gonna crawl, slut," he said, his voice thick and dark, like tar. Then he stalked away.

Tess felt tired again, so tired she wanted to sit down, lie down, go to sleep and not wake up until Butch was an old man in a nursing home somewhere—but forget sitting down; break was over. She picked up the *Rolling Stone* she had dropped on the floor, put it back on the rack, and headed back to her work station. The radio would get her through the day. She listened to the music, drummed with her fingers on the boxes of grapefruit she was opening, ignored Butch. In her experience that was the best way to deal with a nuisance—ignore it.

Her mistake was to think that Butch was just a nuisance.

He got off work the same time she did. And Kam was not out back waiting for her. No reason why he should be. Probably staying out of the rain like a sane person.

But Tess wished he were there. What a pukey day.

It had stopped raining, finally, but the air felt chilly dank. After checking for Kam, Tess slipped back inside and hid out in the women's bathroom while Butch left, then hung around the IGA back room till she was sure he was gone, not waiting for her in the soggy dusk out back—but then she didn't hang around any longer. She thought of going home by the roads, where there were people in houses, people in cars, but nah. Too long, and she was too tired, and she hated to give in to a bully anyway. She walked out of town, then down through the salvage yard the way she usually did.

Hearing nothing but the sound of clammy wind through dead cars. Weeds whispering. A rusty hinge creaking.

All alone.

Then for the first time all day her brain kicked in and she realized she should have been anywhere else.

Stark staring awake now. She moved as fast as she could. No music going in her head that night. She kept scanning woods and brush in all directions, on the lookout—but they didn't try to hide. When she got halfway down the salvage yard she saw them waiting at the bottom, all studly like a row of fence posts.

No way! She had expected Butch himself, not him and all his friends. Tess took off, sprinting behind a row of dead cars piled up like rusty fish, knowing she couldn't outrun them, looking for a place to hide. Hot with fear, she knew she didn't have much time, because she heard them yell—they had seen her.

Moving fast, she was also thinking fast, and the thoughts were not pleasant: hide in some old Buick or panel van? They would just find her and drag her out.

The junkyard shack. She ran to the door, and it wasn't locked—it didn't even have a lock on it, because there was nothing of value in there except maybe a coffeemaker. She lunged inside and closed the door and leaned against it, looking for something to pile against it besides herself.

In a back corner she saw an old armchair with the stuffing spilling out like guts. She darted to it.

Then she heard the door open.

Facing the chair in the dark corner Tess thought hazily of stair rails; why were there no stair rails for her to hide behind? She straightened up, taut, at bay. She turned.

Butch stood in the doorway, menacing, silhouetted, with an ugly little gun in his lifted hand.

"Get out here," he ordered.

Tess screamed.

Not because of Butch. He couldn't make her scream just by showing her a gun. But she screamed because—

The—man, it was Butch in the doorway, she knew it was Butch, yet she was seeing—the nightmare man—

But it was confused, all confused. The blond husky one in the door should have had a knife, and the one getting up from the chair in the dark corner should have had the gun, and he was saying, *Get out, get out, I'm warning you,* and—how dare he, how dare he—kill . . .

Fear hit like a red explosion, she couldn't think, she couldn't move, it was all shards and sparks swirling around, Butch's face, gun, hate, knife, anger, the yelling, the hot smell, that other—beloved face—

Then, like fire shifting, the shards fell together.

She remembered.

She screamed. Remembering hurt so badly that she had to scream, but not just with pain—the anger was worse. Anger, searing through her and turning her to flame. Tess screamed with white-hot fury and lunged straight at the gun.

10

Butch shouted and staggered back as Tess jumped him—and then there was a bang that should have stopped the world.

Tess went berserk.

The bullet just grazed her arm. The next instant Tess knocked Butch flat, so smoking incandescent raging mad that she snatched the gun out of his hand and hit him on the head with it. His gang just stood there not making a sound. Tess was making enough noise for everybody involved. She charged at them—they jumped back from her, faces stony sweating white, and she ran through them. Then she just kept going, though she wasn't running away. She was running to somebody.

She was running to the only person who would listen, and help, and keep her sane. She was running to Kam.

Out of the salvage yard and halfway through the sawmill yard she realized she still held Butch's gun in her hand—no wonder they had all flinched away from her. Probably they had thought they were dead. Tess started to laugh, but it was not a good laugh. She flung the gun down so hard it went off again, could have killed her. So what. Sounded good. She wanted to do it again, but her momentum kept her running, down through the lumberyard and the woods.

Then suddenly she was bone tired. Couldn't run anymore. She just wanted to lie down and die. But she had to keep going, so she did, walking down the overgrown pasture in the dusk. After the rainy day the twilight seemed the color of tarnished silver, but there was still enough of it for her to find her way along the patches of soft spring grass between the rocks and cedars and sassafras and honeysuckle tangles. To keep herself going Tess was trying to be calm, like the pasture, quiet, like the muted light—and thank God, Kam was there in his cowshed camp. As she got near it she could hear his radio going.

> *Out past the pollution*
> *out beyond the fear*
> *out beyond the shadows*
> *shines a secret star . . .*

Crux. But the bullet scratch on Tess's arm felt like somebody had pressed a red-hot knife there, it hurt clear to her toes, and her heart hurt even worse than the wound did, and the song couldn't help her. She started running again. "Kamo!" she cried.

The music stopped. Another few strides and she could see Kam standing in front of his shed, staring toward her, his shoulders stiff, his face—frightened?

He heard calamity in her voice, probably. And he was right. What she had to say was terrible, and too heavy for her to hold by herself. She needed somebody to help her bear the weight.

"Kamo,'" she cried, running up to him. "Kam—I remember. Oh, my God, he killed him. Daddy killed my father."

Tess sat in Kam's shelter on his folded-up blankets, shaking so hard she couldn't walk. Some kind of reaction. Shock. Kam had the campfire going and was heating water in a pot for washing, for her arm. He was worried about her arm. Worried about her—she could tell from the way he kept looking at her.

Shock, or maybe rage. "I won't go back there," she was saying over and over. "I never want to see him again, I never want to talk to him again. I hope his wheelchair gets in the way of a Mack truck. I hope the roof falls in on him. Kam, take me with you." She could just barely talk, yet couldn't stop—she had been babbling since she got there. "Please, wherever you're going, just take me. I'll go with you."

Kam came over and kneeled by her and checked the strip of cloth he had tied tightly around her arm. He had ruined a good T-shirt to bandage her arm. Now he ripped another strip off and tied it over top of the other one, because the first one was soaked with blood.

"He should have told me," she said. "He never told me any of it."

Kam had not said a word. He just lifted his face to her, listening to her, although she had said most of this already.

"I was watching from the stairs," she said. "I saw the whole thing. I saw my father coming in the door, and I—I wanted to run and hug him, but I couldn't. Daddy was sitting in the big armchair—"

It was hard to understand it was him. He wasn't her Daddy then, just her mother's new husband. But she could see his face in the memory. Younger, more hair, but it was him.

"He told my father to get out, but my father kept coming. Daddy told him again, but my father still kept coming. Then Daddy got up and shot him. He shot him. He killed him." Her voice had gone high and shrill. "He killed him. I saw him lie there and die. And then—" She choked to a stop. New memories were crowding in. She hadn't remembered this part when Butch winged her.

"Go on," Kam said quietly.

He was like a pool without a ripple. She could tell him—she had to tell somebody right away or go crazy. "My mother," she whispered.

"Your mother?"

"She saw. She was hiding in the kitchen, and she ran

in, and saw—saw him lying there—and there was only a little blood, I still thought he was just drunk or something—but she—"

The kid sitting on the stairs had gripped the stair railings, and Tess was not a kid anymore but she still needed something to hang on to. She was reaching toward Kam with her shaking hands. He took them and held them, and he was as solid and steady as a young tree.

"She took the gun—from Daddy." She could just barely say this. "She shot him." She could see it now, she had the memory back, but it was like watching TV with the sound off. She couldn't hear the gun fire—she just saw Daddy slump down when her mother pointed the gun at him. It felt like watching Mommy shoot a stranger. Yet—it was Daddy. "She shot Daddy." It was like watching a dream that didn't make much sense, the way she took the gun and he didn't even try to stop her. Then, God, it got worse. "Then she—she killed herself." Tess's mind wasn't quite letting her see this. Just a black explosion, a red scream, Mommy on the floor with—blood. "She put the gun in her mouth and she killed herself."

In front of Tess. Hadn't known she was there. None of them had noticed her. She closed her eyes so she wouldn't see the craziness anymore, the three of them, the gun, but she was still seeing it. She felt Kam let go of her hands and put his arms around her instead.

"Godalmighty," she said, babbling, "it's me that screamed."

She felt Kamo's head on her shoulder, his eyelashes blinking against her neck.

Wet. He was crying.

"Kam?" She put her arms around him. "Do you think—was it your father too?"

He pulled back so he could see her and shook his head like he didn't think so, though his voice came out husky. "What did he look like?"

Her father. It was almost worth all this dithering and shaking to remember him, a mighty palomino god. "Big and blond. Handsome."

"Dyed blond, maybe?" Kam's voice had gone taut.

"No. He was blond all over."

Kam shook his head and looked down at the ground. "My father was dark."

She let her hands drop away from him. Not trembling any longer, just limp and dead-feeling. They sat there.

"Damn," Tess said.

He looked up at her with a flicker of a smile, rubbed his face to dry it, then stood up and went to fetch the pot of water from the fire.

The warm water soothed her hurt arm. The bleeding had mostly stopped, and the wound was just a shallow two-inch gouge. After he had soaped it and rinsed it Kam tied one more bandage around it and let it alone.

Her shaking had stopped. But not her anger.

"Graham crackers?" Kam offered.

"I'm not hungry."

He crouched and looked at her. "You feeling okay to walk home now?"

"I told you, I'm not going back there. Not ever."

He sat cross-legged and looked at her some more. "A few things aren't real clear to me," he said finally. "Like, you said you wanted to hug your father when he came in the door, but you couldn't. How come?"

She didn't even have to close her eyes to see him in the doorway, haloed in light. Big. Blond. Handsome.

With a big ugly fishing knife in his clenched hand.

With words a ten-year-old girl didn't fully understand coming out of his mouth.

Kam asked, "Why was your mother hiding in the kitchen?"

Because she was afraid.

Same reason Tess had been hiding behind the stair railings.

"He was—drunk, maybe," she whispered. "He was—being ugly. He had a knife."

"Threatening Mr. Mathis?"

Tess couldn't remember the ugly words. Just Daddy telling her father to get out. "Maybe."

"Then—when Mr. Mathis shot him—it was self-defense."

Maybe. But it didn't seem to make much difference. "I still hate him," she said. "He should have told me."

Kam puffed his lips like he was getting exasperated. "Look, Tess—as far as I can see, your stepfather must

— 103 —

walk on water. Your father comes in and threatens him, your mother shoots him, he ends up in a wheelchair, and he raises you? He's disabled, with practically no income, yet he keeps you instead of sticking you in an orphan home or something? What's that sound like to you?"

She sat silent.

Kam said, "It sounds like love to me."

She couldn't say a word.

He said, "I'll trade places with you, Tess."

"Go ahead. I'm not going back." Her voice wavered. "I don't care if my father was a mean sleaze, Daddy still shouldn't have killed him."

"Tess . . ."

"I'm mad, damn it!"

"Try being mad at the jackass who did that to you," Kam said, gesturing at her arm.

"Butch?" She had told him about Butch, but now she rolled her eyes. "He's a pants-wetter, he's still shaking. Forget him. I'm so mad at—at the world, I guess. . . ."

"Try to get past the anger," Kam said.

"How?"

It was dark, and the spring peepers were talking. The only light on Kam's face was firelight, and in that warm light his eye shone, his rugged face glowed, he was beautiful—how, Tess wondered, could she ever have thought that he was ugly? He had broad shoulders, wise brows, a heartbreaker smile. He was smiling it now. Yet he knew all about anger. He had better reasons to be angry than she did.

"How do you get past the anger?"

She meant him, personally, and he knew it. He shrugged. "I cry."

He was so brave. She gazed at him.

He said, "Did you love your father, Tess? The blond sleaze?"

Oh, God damn him. Oh, God damn it.

Then the tears came.

Benson Mathis knew at once that something was wrong, because when Tess came in she didn't speak to him and didn't look at him and didn't give him a chance to ask what was the matter, just rushed to her room and shut the door. Then Kam came in, and Kam looked at him, a quiet, steady look.

"She remembers," Kam said.

Benson Mathis let out a long breath. Now that it had finally happened, he was very calm. Tess was in the house; there was a chance that it would be all right. He would get to talk with her. "She remembers everything?"

Kamo sat down across from him and looked levelly at him.

Ben Mathis had to know. "She remembers about her father?"

"Yes."

"And—" Suddenly he couldn't quite say it.

Kam said it for him. "Her mother shot you before she killed herself."

Ben Mathis nodded. "Is Tess—is she talking about leaving?"

"I think she'll be okay once she gets some sleep."

Benson Mathis was no fool. He noticed that Kam had not really answered him, and he knew what that meant. He swallowed, then said, "Kamo—thank you for bringing her back."

He saw that he wasn't the only one having trouble with this; the hard-looking youngster actually blushed. Ducked his head. After a minute the kid said to the floor, "Well—I was barking up the wrong Rojahin. I should go away and let you alone."

"Son, you come around here whenever you want."

His head came up, and his smile was almost worth the trouble.

Kids. More and more Benson Mathis realized they came and went like butterflies, visitors in the life. For the past four years it had been Tess, Tess, Tess, but four years was just a drip-drop in the ocean of time. When she grew up and left, or when she fell in love and left, or even if she yelled that she hated him and left—it would hurt, but his life would go on.

He asked, "What set her off? Did something happen?"

"Oh. Yeah, some jerk she works with has been bothering her." Kam stood up to go.

Benson Mathis frowned. "Bothering her?"

"He won't be bothering her anymore. She took care of him." Kamo headed for the door. "And I plan to take care of him some more." Then he hesitated with his hand on the doorknob, looking over his shoulder. "You okay, man?"

"Sure."

Kam nodded and left.

Benson Mathis sat up in his wheelchair all night. Did not sleep.

Tess slept as if she had been knocked on the head. No nightmares, no dreams. But when she woke up the next morning she felt dead. She didn't want to get out of bed.

Her old windup clock said five till ten. Daddy had let her sleep, as if it weren't a school morning or there was a funeral or something.

She lay there.

After a while she heard thumping noises—Daddy's wheelchair bumping against her door as he tried to open it. A pulpy scraping sound as one of his footrests put yet another gouge in the wood. She pulled the blanket up to her neck as he got the door under control and rolled in.

At the sight of his familiar, ordinary face—weary, careful—her unfamiliar rage blazed. "Get out of here!" She turned away so she wouldn't have to look at him. "Let me alone."

He did not go away. Instead he wheeled over to the

bed and put his hand on her face, stroking the hair back from her eyes.

His gentleness hurt. She lashed out as if he had touched her with a branding iron. Her hand smacked his arm. "Get away!" She lunged out of bed, but he rolled back to keep her from getting out the door.

"Tess. Listen to me." His voice quavered. "I know how you feel—"

The hell he did. "You killed my father!"

"I had to. He was trying to kill me. Tess, the jury acquitted me. It was self-defense."

Some sane portion of her was trying to combat the anger, trying to be fair. Had Daddy done anything so terribly wrong? But the hurt-child portion of her didn't want to hear it. "You should have told me!"

"Couldn't, Tess. When it happened—it set you back bad. Real bad. You wouldn't talk to nobody. You just clawed and bit and screamed. I was afraid they were going to take you away from me, put you in a home or something."

There was a ragged edge of emotion in his voice. Tess stood staring down at him. "Why didn't you let them?" she asked a little less harshly.

"Tess, you were all I had." His voice hitched, stuck on the words. "Still are."

She stood stiffly in her sleep clothes, eyeing him.

"I didn't help you as much as I should have," he said. "I was in a wheelchair, feeling sorry for myself. I should have done more for you than I did."

Tess knew damn well he had done the very best he could. Knew it and didn't want to admit it. She said nothing.

"So you handled it your own way," Daddy said. "You just quit remembering, and all of a sudden you were better. And once you buried it—I was scared to dig it up again." He looked at the floor. "I knew you blamed me."

She knew she shouldn't keep blaming him. Yet she wondered if she would ever be able to stop. The anger just wouldn't let go.

"Get out of my way," she told him.

He did not move except to stare up at her, his round face taut. "Where are you going?"

She pushed past him, muttering, "Going to try to handle it better this time."

11

She took it to the drums. It seemed like music was the one thing in her life she could always count on. She spent the day at the drums, and the drums ate up the anger and liked it.

They helped her sort things out. At first the bad memories kept playing over and over like a videotape—bang, bang, gunshots. Bang, bang, dead on the floor. But later, other memories started bubbling up with the drumbeats. Paradiddle, Yankee Doodle, *riding a pony on the fourth of July.* Soft-shoe brushes on the snare, *Mommy brushing my long blond hair.* Tess could remember her mother's voice, her mother's smile. That was worth something.

Daddy stayed away from her until afternoon, then wheeled into the living room and asked her whether she wanted some lunch. She shook her head.

"You feeling any better?"

"Some," she admitted. She put down the drumsticks

for a moment and looked at him. "What was my father like?"

He hesitated, but then told it to her straight. "He was a dangerous man." His eyes scanned her face as he talked. "Jealous. Violent. Never accepted that Teresa left him. While he was in jail it was okay, but the minute he got out—he was in my house. Busted in. Coming at me with the knife."

"He was in jail?"

"He was in jail a lot. Doing things that might land him in jail was kind of his profession."

"Oh."

"That's how I knew—when Kamo came here—see, Rojahin is the name on your birth certificate, but God knows what the guy's real name was. He went by Marcus Rojahin, Mark Rojohn, John Ryan, uh, Rory Jones, Rory Jamison—a bunch more I can't remember. I figured it was a pretty good bet he wasn't Kamo's dad."

"Great," Tess muttered. "My father was a criminal."

"He was big," Daddy said quietly, "and good-looking, and exciting, and he never did a bad thing to you or Teresa, though sometimes he scared her. That's why she left him. But she always loved him better than me."

The matter-of-fact way he said it made her gawk at him. He answered her stare for a moment, then wheeled away and left her alone with her drums.

Bang, bang. How had it felt when she shot him down?

When Tess finally headed toward her room to get out of her sweatpants and into some real clothes he was sitting in there waiting for her. "I don't want you to go to work today."

Anger flared again. She pushed past him to get to her dresser. "Don't you try to tell me what to do!"

"No. Tessie, listen." He said it more softly. "I don't want you to go."

Then somehow for a moment she actually understood that he was not trying to order her around, that he was worried. More: frightened.

Yet she could not look at him, and her voice insisted on coming out rough. "I'll be back."

"Tess—"

"Look, I'm doing the best I can. I'll be back."

She had to go to work. Butch would think it was on account of him if she stayed away, and partly it would have been on account of him, and she wasn't going to lose a job because an ignorant no-neck male with an attitude had hassled her. In flannel shirt and jeans and her old Red Wings she started hiking toward the IGA.

Walk, walk. When she was in kindergarten, Mommy used to walk her to school. *Hey, I've got memories!* Of walking to school past the fancy-painted fire hydrant on the corner and the big dogs behind a spiky fence— Mommy would growl back at them. Mommy was goofy and a lot of fun, with jars and jars of pink bubble stuff so she and Tess could run around in the back yard blowing bubbles. Laughing at the big ones. Mommy was like a big kid.

Walk, walk. Daddy, the big blond daddy, walking in the door. See what kind of mood he's in. If it was a good one, he'd grab Tess and tickle her just long enough to make her laugh. If it was a bad one, she'd go to her room.

She was a kid then. Not a kid anymore. Too big now to stay away from a stud in a bad mood.

But when she got to the IGA, Butch wasn't there. "Called in sick, said he had a headache," Lupe told her.

"I bet he does," Tess said. She had clobbered him pretty good.

So that was one good thing: no Butch. The memories were another good thing. Yet, trying to do her job, Tess felt miserable. Grieving. As if somebody had died. Well, somebody had: her father, her mother, years ago—but it felt like yesterday. That on top of Butch and his gun on top of all the usual worries: no money, Daddy's health, maybe having to move, school—Tess ached. Her whole chest felt empty with just wanting—something. Wanting to be done wanting.

Crux came on.

> *In this dirty world*
> *you can't see far*
> *but you gotta believe*
> *there's a secret star . . .*

Yeah, right, Tess thought. She didn't want to believe anything anymore. She didn't want to dream anymore. Believing, dreaming—they hurt too much. She threw down the potatoes she was sorting, strode past Lupe, and whacked off the radio.

When she got out of work, Kam was not there.

Tess looked all around, peering into the dusk. She'd thought for sure Kamo would be there. Where was he? He knew she was going through all kinds of crap. She couldn't believe he wasn't there for her.

But he wasn't. Tess stood by the Dumpster, darkness coming, shifting from one big foot to the other, alone again.

Can't depend on anybody.

She pressed her lips together and started walking, out the gravel lot to the alley, up the alley toward the street. Staring at the ground. Tired. Too damn many hills. Kam was probably loafing in his camp, the slug. Listening to Crux on his radio.

Wait a minute. She remembered a couple of times when she had run to his camp in the night and thought she heard a radio, but she'd never seen any—

A car roared up behind her, slowed beside her. Someone laughed.

She turned her head, startled, afraid for a moment. But no, it wasn't Butch. One of his friends, in a thunderous old Barracuda. "Hey!" he yelled at her. "You going to the fight?"

She gawked at him. He laughed again and roared off.

Fight? What was he talking about?

Why had he laughed?

Tess walked, head up, alert now. Just as she reached the end of the alley, Butch's truck whizzed by, headed up Main Street. Butch hadn't seen her, but she had seen him.

Oh, God. Why had that kid yelled something about a fight at her? Why had he laughed? Only one possible reason.

Only one good reason why Kam hadn't been at the IGA to meet her.

Tess started to run up the steep Main Street hill. When her chest hurt, she kept running. When her lungs caught fire, she kept running.

She got to the top just in time to see Butch's truck disappearing down the lane that led to the salvage yard.

Made sense. Of course they'd meet there. Of course they'd do it at dusk, when the men who worked there were gone.

Oh, God. Oh, Kam.

Tess ran. Across somebody's yard and into woods, trying to get to the salvage yard faster. But a creek had cut a ravine in the hillside and the ravine was filled with blackberry tangles. Tess swore, tore through the brambles, ran through the rocky shallow water, lunged up the far side of the ravine. At the top was a tumbledown stone wall topped with a strand of rusty barbed wire; Tess felt it rip her shirt and slice into her back as she dove through. "Damn it!" *Kamo, what kind of stupidity is going through your head?* "Idiot!" She knew some of what he was thinking. At one point after all hell broke loose he had asked her, with that tight lost look on his face, "Did you like Butch? Ever?" and she had almost laughed. No, she hadn't liked Butch. She had wanted Butch to like her. There was a difference.

Kamo, please. Don't get yourself hurt.

She barreled over the hill and down toward the salvage yard, bleeding.

Panting, she reached the edge of the woods.

Then she stood still, feeling her heart clench. Two of Butch's friends were holding Kamo by the arms while the others gathered around. Tess saw the guy who had laughed at her. And she saw Butch strutting and showing off his muscles in front of Kamo. And she heard him.

"You thought we'd slow-dance, maybe?" Butch was yelling. "I got news for you, baby. Nobody calls me out. Nobody." He backhanded Kam across the face.

Kam did not flinch from the whack. He stood straight and still—a stance Tess remembered from the first day she had met him—his face hard, not acknowledging the blow, his body hard and alert, poised like a slim dark knife blade, ready to strike in any direction in an instant. He did not posture or thrust his chest out the way Butch was doing or tug against the hands gripping him. He just stood like flint and said nothing. Butch was not worth answering.

Tess felt dizzy with fear. There were six of them. Too many.

She had to do something.

Get moving.

She ran, carefully and quietly this time. Instead of running toward them she circled around, still in the woods. They were standing in a weedy clearing amid junk, near the shack where Butch had pulled a gun on her. Kam had probably picked the place. The idiot. Gutsy fool.

Leaving the cover of the woods, Tess crouched behind junked cars and scuttled closer.

"—gonna wish you never come here," Butch was threatening. "You want to go now? You ask nice, maybe I'll let you go. Get down on your knees. Say please."

From where she was, behind a wrecked Dodge and almost behind Kam, Tess could not see his face but she could see the taut lines of his shoulders, waiting. He said nothing, but she could tell he was not about to say please. He had no intention of begging. She could tell: all he needed was a chance.

"I said on your *knees*, freak face!" Butch grabbed Kam's headband like he was yanking somebody by the tie. The stitching snapped, the eye patch came off in his hand, and Tess saw Kam's hard shoulders wince as if that hurt him worse than being hit. His fists clenched so hard he shook. For the first time he tried to pull free, lunging toward Butch.

Butch snarled and coiled to punch. They all yelled. Fight! They all piled into Kamo at once.

But not before Tess Mathis, the biggest, strongest girl in Canadawa High School, yelled and charged.

Half a second before they reached Kam she bulled in with her shoulder down and rammed one of the guys holding Kamo in the hollow of his back. She flattened him, and out of the corner of her eye she saw Kam tear away from the other one—she knew all he needed was a chance. He leveled the guy with one good punch while Tess plowed on through and butted her head into Butch's gut. She heard the whoosh as Butch deflated. While he stood there struggling for breath, she punched him in the face.

"Bitch!" He hit back, catching her on the side of the head pretty hard. Tess still felt like she could take him—but things got busy and confused for a while. Forget Butch. She had to concentrate on staying alive, staying on her feet, not letting them get her down where they could kick her. She had to punch straight, kick hard, chomp down on whatever got too close, scream—she screamed like a psycho. Done right, screaming is fighting too.

But she was like Kam; she didn't usually fight unless she had to. And she'd sure never fought six guys at once. They were slowing her down—

She felt somebody put his back against hers to keep them from coming at her from behind. "You all right, Kam?" she yelled.

"Compared to what?" he yelled back. He was okay. He sounded mad.

Kam fought as though he knew what he was doing. And by now Tess had a further opinion of Butch and his friends. They were chicken. She could see it in their eyes. They didn't like actually having to fight instead of just beat up on somebody. Some of them were starting to pull back. They sure weren't worth being afraid of.

"Cowards!" Tess screamed at them—Kam was mad, but she was white-fire nuclear-fission mad. Ballistic. Furious. Fighting felt good, burning the anger out of her. "C'mon! We'll whip the whole bunch of you!"

Then for a moment she was afraid they would take her up on it. But they hesitated, looking over their shoulders. A car was coming down the salvage-yard lane, and she couldn't see much in the dusk with the headlights making her squint but it looked like a Caprice, which is what a lot of Pennsylvania cops drive.

Butch ran for his truck.

"Tess." Kam's voice sounded strained. "Come on." He touched her arm, and she ran after him, into the woods. On his wild black hair she saw blood.

12

No one followed. Tess looked back; Butch and his friends were busy piling into their turbo-powered smoke-in-your-face macho-mobiles and tearing out of there as the police car slewed around and swooped after them.

Fifty feet into the woods Kamo stopped running and walked, not too steadily. Tess walked beside him. "Damn them," Kam said, his voice stretched thin and taut. "I never expected six of them."

"You're an idiot," Tess said.

"I know I am. God damn them." Kam was bleeding. His head, his face, his hands. He was shaking in reaction to the fight. Without its eye patch his face looked strange and naked to Tess. Walking on his left side, his blind side, she couldn't help looking at the place where his eye should have been, and he was too stunned from the fight to notice at first—but then he slammed his hand over that side of his face and turned his head away.

"Kam." She stepped in front of him, halting him. "Stop that." Gently she took his bloodied hand and tugged it down from his face. "You think you're ugly? You're not."

What he was trying to hide was just a scar, that was all. No blind staring withered eye, no empty eyelids, no eye socket, just scarring. A hollow, and on the skin, white lines that formed a crooked cross.

"You're beautiful," she said. So very beautiful. Far more beautiful than her first dream of the secret star had been. Far more brave. A quiet drumming started in her heart, a quiet singing in her bones.

"Crux," she whispered.

She should have known when she heard him singing in the night. Of course the secret star was Kam. Of course Kamo was the secret star. Kamo was the most secret star person who had ever lived.

He gasped. She saw it hit him, stagger him like a gut punch—he knew exactly what she was talking about, and he didn't pretend not to, but it seemed to knock him breathless for a moment. Tess exclaimed, "Kam, it's all right!" She put out her hands to steady him by the shoulders.

She felt him quivering like a guitar string. "Are you—going to—tell—"

"Of course not." She could never do that to Kam. In

a way he was strong, but she knew well enough why he hid behind his music; in a way he was the most frail person she knew. Scarred, scared, shy, dreaming, crying sometimes—if the newspeople got hold of him, they would eat him for dinner. Headlines—STAR MUTILATED AS CHILD. WANDERING STAR SEEKS LONG-LOST FATHER. Photographers following him everywhere, fans mobbing him—it would kill him. Tess felt annoyed at herself for blurting out the word that had jolted him so much. After he had just taken on Butch for her sake, yet. Crazy fool. As if she couldn't take care of herself.

She said, "It's okay, Kam. Look, you may be Crux, but you're still an idiot."

That wrenched a noise out of him, a yawp that might have been either a sob or a laugh. "Tess—" He threw his arms around her and hugged her hard. She felt his chest heave.

"For God's sake," she complained even though she was hugging him back—it had been a rough couple of days, and she didn't feel as though she could take too much more. "Don't cry." She patted him, but it was more like she was whacking at his back to make him stop. "Kam, c'mon."

He put his head up and looked at her, wet eyed; tears ran down his bloodied cheek into his shaky smile. "Tess—you are beautiful. You are the most beautiful person on the face of the planet."

Oh, *sure*. She rolled her eyes and started walking again. Kam walked beside her, down past the sawmill.

Then through more woods. Then out of the woods, down the abandoned pasture toward the creek. Good. Cold water on cuts and bruises. Cold water would help Kam.

"You shouldn't be fighting," Tess grumbled at him. He was still trembling. His face was bruised, his mouth was swelling, his hands were bleeding. "You're a musician, not a fighter. What if you—"

Kam said, "I'm fine." But he didn't sound fine.

"Look at your hands. What if you messed up your hands?"

"I'm fine, Tess!"

They walked down a cow ledge to the river bottom then along the creek trail, looking for a place where they could get through the brush to the water.

Kam said, "I'm used to being beat up."

"That don't make it right." Though in a way, Tess knew, it did factor in. Crux. The white scar, hidden. The hidden pain. He had named himself after the pain.

He said, "You're a musician too. What are you doing fighting?" He sounded okay now. Tess looked at him, and he glanced back at her with a shadowy smile.

She said, "I wish I was half the musician."

"Shush." He flushed and looked away.

They came to an opening between sumac clumps where cows had trampled a way down to the creek years before. "C'mere." Kam took Tess gently by the arm and steered her to a seat on a big weeping-willow root right at the creek bank. He squatted down, stripped off his T-shirt and dipped it in the water and pressed it to her face.

Until that minute Tess hadn't noticed her face was a mess. The cold creek water burned, and Kam's faded blue T-shirt came away from her red with blood. He sopped it in water again and dabbed gently, intent on her. It was getting late—the light was low and mellow, like muted trumpet music, and that golden glow lighting up the scarred side of his face made him look like a rough-cut angel.

He said, "I just wanted to sell a song. That's all, just get the song out where people could hear it. But—this agent—he liked the way I sang it on the tape I sent him. I told him I didn't want to do concerts and tours and all that crap. And once he got a look at me, I guess he could see I wasn't any heartthrob."

"Like you have to be?" Her tone was sharper than it should have been. But he looked up with that wide, warm, heartbreaker smile of his, as if she had said something wonderful.

"Well, yeah. He thought so. But he hated to pass on the song, so he said okay, let's try something." Kam's smile went wry, and he looked away, crouching there with the wet cloth dripping down between his feet. "I thought maybe I'd make a couple of bucks."

"So you made a couple million," Tess said.

"No. Not that much. But enough." He reached up to sop at her face some more.

But she took the wet cloth from him and started soaking the blood out of his hair. He was still trembling some. "C'mere," she ordered. "They did something to your head."

He let her look. It wasn't so bad. A bump. He let her clean up his face.

Then he ducked his head. He said, "Tess, I know you've got to be wondering why the—why I haven't helped you out."

With money, he meant. "Hush." But her voice came out harsh because yeah, the thought was starting to occur to her and she hated it. As if he hadn't given her enough. She stood up to get away from herself. "C'mon."

She led him up the pasture to his camp and started making a fire for him. He hung his wet shirt on a rope strung under the overhang and sat in the dirt, searching in a knapsack. He pulled out a shirt and put it on. He rummaged deep, then pulled out a spare eye patch and started to slip it over his head.

"Don't," Tess said.

With his hands in midair he peered at her.

"Don't put it on," she said. She liked the balanced look of his bare face, scars and all. Fire was leaping up from kindling and newspaper. She looked at him in the warm light.

"Huh," he said, and he laid the eye patch aside. "Hungry?"

"No." Her stomach felt tense, like the rest of her, still clenched from the fight.

"Neither am I."

They sat. Silence. Tess fed sticks to the fire and knew there was another reason she felt knotted up like a pretzel.

Finally she mumbled, "Okay, why?"

"Why what?"

Why hadn't he slipped some cash to her and Daddy, she meant. But she said, "Why are you living like a drifter?"

He looked up at the sky as if it could help him answer.

The evening was full of stars. It was the white-flower time of spring—blackberry blossom, cow lily, wild rose. Down in the creek bottom purple nightfall had gathered, thick with the smell of the white flowers, and they looked up from the dark ground to the darkening sky like stars, and maybe the real stars looked back.

"It's what I'm used to," Kam said. That sounded lame, even to him. He shook his head. "I dunno, Tess. It's hard for me to sing in a house. I have one now—I even spent this past winter there. But—I need to get out under the sky. Look up at the stars."

Made sense.

More silence.

As if he had heard the rest of what she was thinking Kam said, "I give pretty much all the money straight to the Children's Defense Fund. I don't want it. Don't trust it."

"I'll take it," Tess joked. Though no joke is ever really a joke.

He turned to her stark serious. "Tess, you don't know how much I've thought about giving you a wad of it. But listen, is that what you really want? Some hotshot riding in and tossing a bundle of thousand-dollar bills out the limousine window?"

"Sure, I'd like that," she said—but her voice quavered, uncertain, because somehow money seemed less important than it had a few days before. Too much had happened. Was money going to help her love Daddy again? Was money going to make her pretty so some jackass like Butch would like her?

Couldn't depend on anybody, she'd decided. Forget dreams. Was money what she wanted instead?

"Tess, you don't know." Kamo's eye had gone narrow and hard and dark as the valley shadows. "Money's poison," he said, his voice low. "It kills any real understanding between people."

She didn't say anything, but she knew it was true. She knew because she could feel the thought of money trying to work its poison right that minute.

"I've seen money in action." Kam looked away from her, staring into the dusk. "My stepfather had money."

Oh. Oh, God. "Kam, it's okay," Tess told him. "Forget the damn money."

"You really understand?

"Yes."

Partly true. She understood that she was in danger of hurting him badly if she wasn't careful. She understood that he needed a friend, not somebody who owed him.

She understood that she had to keep getting stronger.

"Forget I ever heard of money," she said.

He could tell she meant it. His voice settled down, and he was looking at her quiet-eyed again. "You and your daddy going to be okay?"

"Yes." She tried to sound sure. But she wasn't sure at all. She didn't feel like things between her and Daddy were ever going to be the same.

She trudged up Miller's pasture in the dark, her legs aching. Staring at the ground in front of her, she didn't even notice the glow in the sky. But coming over the crest of the hill, she looked up and blinked. It was like facing into the sun.

For a moment she didn't recognize her own house with the lights on. Daddy must have had every light in the place on, including the outdoor lights front and back. Tess could see him sitting in the yard in his wheelchair, waiting for her.

"Power came back on in the middle of the day," he called the minute he saw her. "The refrigerator started a-humming and the pump kicked on and I said, what the hell? Went over to Millers' to call Met-Ed, and they say it's no mistake. The bill's been paid. Now who would have paid it?"

Tess opened her mouth, then closed it again.

"What happened to you?" As she walked closer, he had seen her messed-up face.

"I ran into a brick wall."

"A brick wall with fists?"

She said nothing. It wasn't the first time she had been in a fight. And he sure didn't want to argue with her, what with all that had been happening. He let it go.

"You want some supper?" he asked. "You've got your choice. The Millers dropped off a whole passel of goodies to fill the fridge . . ." He was trying hard to make Tess smile, but she just stood there looking at the lights. His voice trailed away.

Low-voiced, Tess said, "It reminds me of that Christmas Eve when you were working that extra job and didn't get home till late and we waited up for you. Mommy had every light in the place on, and all the Christmas lights, and candles in the windows, waiting for you."

She saw his throat quiver as he swallowed. He didn't say anything.

She said, "What do you mean, she loved him better than she loved you?"

"She did." He was having trouble talking. "Your mama had a heart that don't give up, Tess. She was nuts that way."

"Was she—was she really crazy?"

He shook his head. "Just kind of nuts. And beautiful. I was crazy about her, but she never should have married me. She was too much woman for a guy like me."

Guy like him? There he sat, an ordinary-looking bald man in a wheelchair, and Tess had known him half her life yet she felt all her brain cells bungee-jumping, stretching to believe he could be for real. "She—loved somebody else, and she—blamed you, shot you, almost killed you—and you still loved her?"

"Yes."

"And—you still wanted to keep me?"

Tears shone on his pudgy cheeks. "You were her daughter. I loved you. Still do."

She wanted to hug him. Couldn't quite do it, but she put her hand out to him. He took it and held it in both of his. "We're gonna be okay," he said. His voice rubbed in his throat.

She nodded. "The minute I get paid I'm calling the phone people to get the service put back in."

He nodded and smiled but said, "That's not what I mean. We're gonna be all right. We're family."

How could he sound so sure? Things were never going to be the way they were before, when he had been her capital-*D* Daddy who could do no wrong.

But maybe they shouldn't be. Maybe it was better for her to risk caring about a daddy who could let her down.

She couldn't quite smile back at him. A whisper of leftover anger wouldn't let her. But maybe soon she'd get past that.

Tess took hold of his wheelchair to help him back into the house. "Let's go eat," she said.

13

A couple of days later Tess got up very early, while it was still dark. Ten thousand stars shone down bright as daisies. At four in the morning Tess walked through the woods and down Miller's hill toward the creek bottom.

Almost from the start she'd known Kam would have to go away someday.

She found her way between rocks and little cedars as surely as a cat. Never stumbled. Never strayed. Winding along the creek path, she watched the stars reflected in the black water, like wild lilies floating there.

There was a man named Rojahin living in Eli, Nevada, Kam's missing-persons expert said. Mark Rojahin. About the right age.

Near Kamo's camp, treading between clumps of honeysuckle, Tess did not try to be silent, yet she was. The honeysuckle was starting to bloom already, with a smell sweet as angels, white flowers clustered like stars in the night. But the brightest star lay on the dark ground ahead. She followed its hot golden glimmer and walked up to the embers of Kamo's fire.

He was awake, sitting by the fire, as she had thought he might be.

"Couldn't you sleep?" he asked, his voice ghosting to her soft as a moth.

"You should talk." She sat down opposite him. "You anxious?"

"More—more like I'm holding my breath. I don't dare think about it. Don't dare get my hopes up." She could hear the excitement in his voice, low and vibrant, like distant drums.

"I hope it's him," Tess told him. "Your father. I hope you find him. And I hope . . ." She let the sentence trail away. Couldn't say that she hoped his father would be glad to see him. If that happened, Kam would be so happy he'd forget all about her.

But she wanted that for him anyway. Happiness.

"Tess." He was looking at her the way he had done that first day, his head alert, his single eye narrow. Wondering why she was there. Trying to read her. "Everything okay?"

"Sure."

"Mr. Mathis all right?"

"Yeah." She and Daddy were doing pretty good.

"Something wrong at work? Butch been hassling you?"

"No." Butch was going to military school in a few weeks. Till then, she could handle him.

Silence stretched too long as Kam watched her, wary, almost afraid, as if he thought she might try again to keep him from leaving. He knew darn well there were things on her mind—she had wished he was her brother, he had wished she was his sister; she looked in the mirror and saw his music shining in her eyes; she wished he could stay, he had to go.

He had to go away. And her heart was aching.

But they knew those things. What was the use of saying them?

She said, "Sing for me?"

He gazed back at her and she saw that she had done right. His scarred face softened. His dark eye went wide and soft.

His things were all packed. His wash line gone. Knapsack bulging. Blankets rolled, even the one that he had always kept spread at the back of the cowshed. Tess knew now what he had hidden under it: a guitar. Small, battered and old, its mellow-gold wood glowing in the emberlight, it rested on top of his gear. Kamo reached for it and laid it across his lap.

He did not hold it up the way people usually played a guitar. Instead, he cradled it flat in his lap and pressed his fingers straight down on it to strum a few chords— peculiar chords, minor with a twist that was all his own. Tess had almost forgotten until then about his bent, crooked left hand. He strummed and picked with it, and fingered with his right hand, when most people were taught to do the opposite. But his damaged hand could not have managed the fingering.

So he did not play guitar like anyone else anywhere. Because he came at the strings from a different angle, he had made up his own chords, and they made Tess feel as though music should have been invented that way in the first place. Like she was sitting there watching the god of all guitarists shaping music out of darkness the way God had shaped Adam out of clay—Kam was that good. His fingering hand ran up and down the guitar like fire. He key-changed to major, and the notes flew up like sparks, bright and hot and starry.

He sang.

In the sin-bin city
you can't see far
In the shadows
the bad pose
bullets fly
sirens cry
the blood flows
blows stun
children sob for pity
children cry for pity—
But out beyond the pollution
out beyond the fear

out beyond the shadows
shines a secret star

That incredible voice. It seemed made out of grit and
dreams. She could hear his scarred throat in each
note—it was Kam. Yet it rose to be a cross of air floating above the clouds. It was Crux.

"Drum for me, Tess!" he cried, strumming.

The only drum she had was the earth, and she wasn't
quite strong enough to really make it reverberate. But
she tried. Her hands slapped out the rhythm, trying to
make music out of dirt.

Yet—it wasn't so crazy. Sky and earth belonged together. Stars and dust.

> *Out beyond the clouds*
> *out beyond the fear*
> *out beyond the shadows*
> *shines a secret star*
> *In this dirty world*
> *you can't see far*
> *but you gotta believe*
> *there's a secret star*

Her palms felt on fire with drumming when the song
ended. Kamo laid the guitar aside and leaned back, but
he didn't look tired. He just looked serene. A quiet pool.

"That felt good," he said.

She felt herself smiling at him. Felt the smile start

somewhere deep and bubble up, the way music bubbled up in her.

"Someday," Kam said. A pause. "It may take years." A pause as he looked past her into the years. "But someday, I am going to have the courage. I will stand up and say to people, *I am Kam, I am Crux. They brutalized me, see?* I will not need to hide anymore. I may even take off this stupid eye patch. I will want to say, *Don't let it happen to children anymore.* I will need to say that."

He looked back to her.

"And I will want to play for people. Sing. Be who I am. And I'm going to need a drummer, Tess."

It wasn't a promise, she knew. She would have to be good. Very, very good. But it was a wonderful maybe. It was a hope worth more than any amount of money.

"Tess?"

She managed to get her mouth moving. "I'll try," she whispered.

He sat there looking at her. Then she realized she was seeing him by more than the glow of embers. Hushed light lay soft as a mother's touch on his face. Dawn.

The stars were going out. But she tried not to think of it that way.

"Time for you to get going," she said.

Her saying it released him. He nodded, stood up, kicked dirt over the fire.

"I'll be back every now and then to check on you," he said. "Don't forget."

"I hear you."

"Just when you least expect me. You'll be coming around a bend in the path holding hands with your boyfriend, and there I'll be."

She wrinkled her nose at him. "Get out of here."

He hoisted his knapsack. She got up to help him fasten the blankets on top of it. The guitar hung from a strap around his neck and left shoulder.

Then he stood there.

"Let me know if you find him," she told him.

He nodded. "Bye," he whispered. He turned away.

"Bye."

She had meant to let him go without any more than that. Stand and watch him walk away. If he turned to wave, wave back.

But then she thought of something. "Hey," she called after he had gone a few steps.

He turned to look at her, holding his face still. She looked at him, memorizing him: One eye. Scars. Headband doing nothing to tame his wild black hair. Broad shoulders. Slim strong muscle. Damaged hand.

How did it all add up to so much?

"You've got what you wanted, anyway," she told him.

He swiveled his head, quizzical. "What I wanted?"

She told him, "Somebody loves you."

His face moved like when the wind ripples a still pool. For an eyeblink he looked as if he might cry, but there was no need to cry. Maybe he understood that already.

"Tess," he breathed.

"Get your butt moving," she ordered him.

He turned to wave once, at the top of the hill. She waved back. Then he went striding into the woods, and she could no longer see him.

It was stark, white, too-damn-early daylight. But Tess knew: even when she couldn't see them, the stars were still there. The stars were still there, behind the glare. Like a secret. Like a mystery. Like a hope.

She headed toward home, up the rocky pasture, stomping along, tapping out a rhythm on her leg and getting the music going inside her head and planning how she might scrape together money for drum lessons, how she might hook up with a band. And watching the white trumpet flowers open up, every single one of them tilting toward the sky.